''And when you leave, what then?'' Tracy asked

''Am I to be a brokenhearted lover, jilted at the altar?''

''When the matter has been satisfactorily dealt with, then the truth can be told—that I was merely playing a role,'' Neil replied.

''Not playing it well. You hardly bother to disguise the fact that you despise me. No one will believe for a moment that we have any kind of relationship.''

''They'll believe it.'' Neil brushed her hair lightly back from her face. ''Every person at that party tonight is going to be positive that I'm crazy about you.'' He cradled her chin in a large hand. ''And why not? I'm a man, and you're a very attractive woman, Tracy.''

No one had ever said her name with that husky trace of emotion before. Suddenly panicked, Tracy stepped hastily back. ''Only in public,'' she said desperately.

Jeanne Allan, who was born and raised in Nebraska, lived there until her marriage to a United States Air Force lieutenant. More than a dozen moves have taken them to Germany and ten different states. Between moves Jeanne spent time as a volunteer. With her two teenage children she enjoys nature walks, bird-watching and photography at the family's cabin in the Colorado mountains, and she enjoys all kinds of crafts, including making stained-glass windows. She has always liked to write, but says her husband had to bully her into writing her first romance novel.

Books by Jeanne Allan

HARLEQUIN ROMANCE

2665—PETER'S SISTER
2845—WHEN LOVE FLIES BY
2875—THE WAITING HEART
2899—THE GAME IS LOVE
2935—TRUST IN LOVE
2989—ONE RECKLESS MOMENT

BLUEBIRDS IN THE SPRING

Jeanne Allan

Harlequin Books

TORONTO • NEW YORK • LONDON
AMSTERDAM • PARIS • SYDNEY • HAMBURG
STOCKHOLM • ATHENS • TOKYO • MILAN

Original hardcover edition published in 1989
by Mills & Boon Limited

ISBN 0-373-03073-8

Harlequin Romance first edition September 1990

Printed in U.S.A.

CHAPTER ONE

'But—but—that's blackmail!' Tracy sputtered, jumping up from her chair and staring in anger and astonishment at the two men across the room. Ed Baldwin looked away with an air of embarrassment while the other man regarded her steadily, his hazel eyes full of unmistakable disdain. Tracy ignored him, concentrating on the man more likely to be persuaded. 'Ed, you can't let him do this to me. You know how I feel about that man.'

'That man is your father.' The deep-voiced rebuke was the first time the other man had spoken, having left the previous explanations to Ed.

Tracy whirled, her fists defiantly clenched against her hips. 'Stan Warner was my father.'

One eyebrow rose a fraction of an inch in polite disbelief. 'You mean that Jake Archer was cuckolded?'

She felt the red colour that stung her cheeks. 'It takes more than a biological accident to make a real father.'

He shrugged. 'If you say so.'

'I don't know who you think you are——'

'Neil Charles,' he interrupted smoothly. 'Your new baby-sitter.'

'Over my dead body!'

'Precisely what I'm here to prevent.'

There was no mistaking the amusement in his voice, and Tracy could taste the bitterness which rose in her throat. 'It's not a laughing matter,' she retorted.

'No? You're behaving as though it were a black comedy.'

Deliberately she turned her back to him. 'Ed,' she appealed, 'there must be something I can do.'

Ed fiddled nervously with some papers on his desk, avoiding Tracy's accusing gaze. 'You don't have many options,' he finally observed. 'I thought I had made that clear to you. Your mother made only the one will, shortly after she married Jake Archer, leaving him everything.'

Fuelled by anger, Tracy paced back and forth across the wide expanse of wine-coloured carpeting. 'Grandmother meant the house to be mine.'

'Your mother didn't mean . . . she simply couldn't. . .'

Tracy waved away Ed's halting explanation. 'I know. She wasn't very good at facing anything unpleasant. That's why she never let Stan take out any insurance on her.' She grimaced. 'Meanwhile, I'm flat broke.'

'A new experience for you, I'm sure.'

Tracy spun around to glare at the tall, brown-haired man. 'And what is that supposed to mean, Mr Charles?'

'Along with the rest of the literate world, I know all about you, Miss Archer.'

'Warner,' she bit out between clenched teeth. 'And I can guess your sources. Newspapers,' she said with deep loathing.

He dipped his head in acknowledgement. 'You're the type of juicy titbit they love best. Only twenty-three. Beautiful. The daughter of a rich and successful Wall Street attorney. A rich stepfather. Mother one of the *grandes dames* of Denver society. Fancy school back east. European travels including your latest jaunt to Ireland—to recover from the tragedy, according to the gossip columns. No real job. Dabbles in something artsy-craftsy.' There was an air of detachment about him as he reeled off the information. 'A typical rich, spoiled brat.'

'I see,' Tracy said, shaken by the concise biography. All true. And yet so terribly misleading. She turned away. The window on the far wall usually framed a mountain vista of extraordinary beauty. Today the Rockies were barely visible behind a brown curtain of smog.

'Aren't you going to deny it?'

'This isn't necessary, Charles,' Ed protested. 'Tracy has had a rough enough time these past three months. The Press ate up the scandal. Stan Warner, prominent manufacturer, embezzling from his own firm, murdering his wife, and then committing suicide. Her mother is dead, and even if Warner was not her real father, she's lived with him for years.'

'Pardon me,' Neil Charles said with sarcastic emphasis, 'I missed the grief. I thought she was mourning the fact that she isn't getting the big wad of money she was expecting.'

'I won't do it!' Tracy spat. 'I'd rather be a bag-lady on the 16th Street mall than have this man in my house.'

'Not your house,' Neil Charles interjected.

Ed stood up behind his mammoth desk. 'I'll leave you two alone to discuss your decision.' After a swift look at the other man, he added, 'Of course, you're always welcome to continue your stay with Jess and me, Tracy, but I'd like to caution you against any hasty decisions. You don't have to see your father;

he isn't asking that. Merely go along with his wishes for a month or so, and your grandmother's house and the money are yours.'

The door had no more than closed behind Ed than Neil Charles resumed his attack. 'Now that you've driven away Baldwin and vented your spleen, *Miss Warner,*' his voice derisively underlined her name, 'do you think that we can get on with the business at hand?'

'I'm sorry you're bored,' Tracy began with false cordiality.

'No, you're not, but I am. All your arguing won't change one thing. Jake has you over a barrel, and you know it. Either you accede to his wishes and go out to New York, or you're going to have me glued to your side until this business is settled. Otherwise, you're to be out of the house immediately, and he'll see to it that you'll never see a penny of your mother's money.'

'I don't give a damn about the money!' she raged. 'If my mother had left it all to charity, or even a stranger on the street, I could accept that. What I can't accept is it going to him. He doesn't deserve it.'

'And you do?'

'What right do you have to judge me?' Tracy crossed the office in long, angry strides. 'None. No more right than he has to meddle in my life. I don't want anything to do with him.'

'So you've said. At excessive length.' Neil Charles slouched back in the cushy leather chair, his legs stretched out in front of him. 'Is it so surprising that a father would be concerned for the safety of his daughter?'

'I'd hardly call threatening to steal my inheritance the act of a loving father,' Tracy refuted.

'Perhaps the first requirement of being a loving father is that one has a loving daughter.'

Tracy sucked in her breath at the unexpected blow. What did this man know about being a loving daughter? If she closed her eyes she could still see herself as she'd been that afternoon so long ago. She'd been waiting for her father because they were going to a baseball game. She had a team hat and was wearing her catcher's glove. Her mother had come out, crying, and she had told Tracy that she wasn't going to the game, that her father wasn't coming home, that he didn't love them any more. Tracy could still remember the feeling of disbelief, screaming at her mother that she was lying. Swallowing hard over the painful lump in her throat, she said, 'Jake Archer got exactly the kind of daughter he deserved.'

Apparently he chose not to debate the point, apart from a mocking look of scepticism, as he ostentatiously consulted his watch before rising abruptly from the chair. 'Well? What's it to be? I'm scheduled to call Jake in a few minutes with your answer.'

Tracy sank slowly down into the depths of the enormous, upholstered sofa that lined one wall of Ed's panelled office. 'Now? You want my answer now?' she asked in a shaky voice.

He gave her an impatient look. 'What did you think this meeting was all about? A tea-party?'

'I thought. . .some time. . .maybe a week. . .'

'Why? So you can figure out a way around your father's request?'

'Ultimatum!' Tracy snapped, her jeering voice stiffening her spine and bringing her to the edge of the sofa.

'If you find his request so offensive, tell him to go to hell. If you really don't care about the money. . .'

'I care about the house.' She clenched her fists against the threat of losing it. For years the happiest moments of her life had taken place at the house in Palmer Lake. Memories of summers spent there with adoring grandparents washed over her. She'd always known that some day the house would be hers, and she'd anticipated introducing her own children to the enchanting sight of baby bluebirds, or the fun of seeking out the first pasque-flower of spring. Events that would never come to pass if she refused to accede to Jake Archer's demands. Hot tears stung the underside of her eyelids.

'If it's having a bodyguard that you dislike so much, you could always go out to New York and stay with Jake and his wife.'

'Never!' Tracy jumped to her feet and stumbled across the room to the window, blinded by tears of rage and pain. 'Never! I hate him! He chose to get out of my life years ago, and all I want from him is that he stays out.'

'Tears are a nice touch. Most men would fall on their knees in abject apology, begging your forgiveness, anything to stop your crying.'

Angrily, Tracy dashed the moisture from her cheeks with the back of her hand, as furious with herself for crying as at him for his brutal sarcasm. She could expect no sympathy from him. Sympathy! Since when did Tracy Warner go around begging for sympathy? Pride lent her strength and she turned to face him. 'Then there's no point in wasting my tears on you, is there?' Snatching her bag off Ed's desk, she found a handkerchief and defiantly blew her nose.

'Nope,' he promptly answered her rhetorical question. 'You're young, healthy, beautiful, and, I assume, intelligent, since you're Jake's daughter.' He shrugged. 'You're not the first kid who found out that life was tougher than she'd bargained for. OK, I'll admit that you've had a rough time these past few months. . .'

'Thank you so much,' she said belligerently.

'But I also think,' he continued, disregarding her comment, 'that it's time you quit feeling sorry for yourself because your father left your mother.'

'What would you know about it? Your father was probably Father of the Year eighteen years running.'

'My father died when I was fourteen,' he said flatly. 'He was fixing our TV aerial and fell off the roof.'

The flash of pain in his eyes was gone so quickly that she might have imagined it. 'I'm sorry,' she said impulsively.

'I don't remember asking for your pity.'

'It wasn't pity. It was politeness. Something you obviously have very little acquaintance with.'

'I suppose you think, because you were raised in a fancy house with bushels of money, that you cornered the market on etiquette? Well, let me tell you, Tracy Warner, where I come from it's considered very bad manners to kick a man in the teeth when he attempts to help you.'

'Help? Help! You think that he wants to help. . .?' Her voice was rising in near hysteria, and she choked off the rest of the question and took a deep breath. 'I can see exactly what he's doing. He knows that I'll never go out to New York and live with him. He knows that I don't want some stranger living in my house with me. He wants me to say the hell with him, the hell with the money. Do you know why?'

'I'm sure you're dying to tell me.'

Striding angrily around the office, Tracy ignored his cool sarcasm. 'He hated my grandparents. They were against his marriage to my mother and he never forgave them. He hated that house; hated the outdoors. He probably wants to burn it down. Well, I'll show him!' She whirled to face the man who was leaning against Ed's desk, watching her with eyes that mocked her anger. 'I'll want it in writing. You can live in my house and pretend to be a bodyguard, or whatever you want to call it, but when you're both bored with your silly games the house is mine.' Her emotional tirade over, she sank limply back on to the sofa.

'And the money,' he said drily. 'Don't forget the money.'

Tracy started to deny it, but then mentally shrugged. 'When will you be moving in?'

'Ed told me that you were returning to your home tomorrow. I'll go with you,' he said.

'Fine.' Standing, she walked over to Ed's desk and retrieved her bag. Anger and disbelief had acted as temporary anaesthetics, but now they were wearing off, leaving her reeling under the painful blows of the afternoon's revelations. Murder! She felt physically ill. 'I'll see you tomorrow.'

He stopped her before she could escape. 'Before then.' There was a hint of cruel amusement in his voice. 'I'll be at the Baldwins' party tonight. It will be a good opportunity for you to introduce me around—as your boyfriend.'

'Boyfriend? You?' She spun around, his pronouncement jerking her from her self-pitying thoughts. 'You can't be serious!'

He gave her a peculiar look. 'How did you plan to explain my presence?'

'With the truth.'

'No,' he said sharply. 'Jake wants everyone to continue believing that Stan Warner was a thief and a murderer.'

Tracy swayed from the impact of his blunt words. 'Your social chit-chat must make you a hit with all the ladies in New York,' she said shakily. 'Now, if you'll excuse me, I don't care to stand here and listen to that man's plans for revenge just because Stan married my mother.'

He crossed the room in two giant strides and gripped her shoulders angrily. 'Don't be stupid. If the culprit thinks he's free and clear, he's bound to get careless. Then Jake will pounce.' His fingers tightened on her shoulders. 'Until then. . .in public, we're a pair.'

He was standing too close to her. Overwhelmingly masculine and threatening. She could barely breathe. His dislike of her hung in the air between them, a palpable, living thing. Pretend that she cared for this man? Impossible! Numbly she shook her head. 'I-I can't.'

His lips curled down in scorn. 'Can't? Or won't?'

She shook free of his grasp. 'I can't.' Her mind raced in search of a reason that would convince him. 'Th-think of the gossip. After everything else that's happened. . .to take on a lover. . .'

'Not a lover,' he corrected. 'A fiancé.'

'You're joking?'

'Certainly I'm not. What could be more plausible than the man who loves you and wants to marry you rushing to your side to support you in your time of need?'

'After three months?' she asked. 'Hardly racing.'

'It took me that long to convince you that I love you, and that the scandal didn't matter to me.'

Tracy shook her head again. 'It won't work. No one is going to believe that I would fall in. . .would have a fiancé who. . .'

'Who what?' He frowned, creating a deep gash across his forehead.

Her mouth felt dry. 'Looks at me like that.'

He went perfectly still. 'I wasn't aware that I looked at you any differently from any man seeing a beautiful woman.'

'You know very well that you look at me as if you wish you had a clove of garlic to ward me off, or a cross to hold in front of you. Or are you just watching to see if I'll commit some unspeakable crime, too?' A sudden shocking thought hit her with the force of an unexpected blow to the stomach. 'No, that's not it,' she breathed, gripping her bag hard. 'You think that I've already committed an unspeakable crime. That's it, isn't it? I'm the one you have targeted as the villain. You think I did it!' Her eyes rounded in horror. 'How could you?'

His reaction to her accusation was totally unexpected. He laughed. '"How could you?"' he mimicked. 'I never would have believed that Jake had a fool for a daughter.'

Anger flicked along her veins. 'So far you've categorised me as greedy, an ungrateful daughter, and now a fool. I may be a fool, Mr Charles, but not as big a fool as you are. Regardless of your high opinion of me,' she said sarcastically, 'none of my friends is going to believe that I'm so desperate for a man that I'll put up with one who talks to me the way you do.' She fumbled for the doorknob.

A long arm reached around her and held the door

shut. 'I apologise for my last remark. The fact that you would think that you were under suspicion caught me by surprise. There has never been any question of your innocence. My purpose here is exactly as I said—to ensure your safety. You don't want me, and I don't want to be here, but circumstances have stuck us together.'

'And when you leave, what then? Am I to be a broken-hearted lover, jilted at the altar?'

'When the matter has been satisfactorily dealt with, then the truth can be told—that I was merely playing a part.'

'Not playing it well. You hardly bother to disguise the fact that you despise me. No one will believe for a minute that we have any kind of a relationship.'

'My name is Neil.' He brushed her hair lightly back from her face. 'They'll believe it, Tracy.'

No one had ever said her name with that husky trace of emotion before. Tracy swallowed hard. 'It won't be easy. Two people who dislike each other. . .'

'I'll be on my best behaviour. After tonight, every person at that party is going to be positive that I'm crazy about you.' He cradled her chin in a large hard. 'And why not? I'm a man, and you're a very attractive woman.'

The words uttered in a low, seductive voice caught Tracy offguard and she looked at him in confusion. A slow, sensuous smile spread across his face, accentuating his sudden transformation from accuser to charmer. His chin was still firm, the cheekbones still high, the nose still almost Roman in shape, but lips which had been hard and thin softened in a wide curve disclosing gleaming white teeth, while his hazel eyes were warm pools that enticed her beyond her depth.

Tracy's heart stopped mid-beat only to restart in triple time. The rich smell of the old leather chairs faded away to be replaced by the subtle oriental fragrance of sandalwood. She could no longer hear the faint murmur of voices beyond the door; the only sound was the blood pounding in her ears. Suddenly panicked, she stepped hastily back. 'Only in public,' she said desperately.

Neil's eyes glinted. 'Of course. Starting tonight.'

'I won't be there.'

'Of course you will.' For the first time there was a hint of anger in his voice, as if her little rebellion had previously amused him but now he was tired of their game.

Only it was no game to Tracy. 'Not yet, not tonight.' Still stunned by the shocking revelations, she needed time to restore her equilibrium. She tugged on the door-handle.

'You'll be there,' he said softly.

'Or what?' Tracy demanded, whirling about to face him, her nerves stretched close to breaking point.

'Or I'll drag you there, if I have to dress you myself.'

The words were so soft-spoken, it took a moment before Tracy grasped their threat. Neil was back in the large leather chair, one long leg hooked over the arm, his hands folded across his stomach, his eyelids shut. He looked as if he were half-asleep.

Tracy was not deceived. 'I may be forced to allow you to be my bodyguard, but I will not be dictated to. Do you understand?'

He slowly opened his eyes. His face totally expressionless, he took in Tracy's defiant stance, and then his eyes swept her body in a gaze so loaded with sensuality that she couldn't have been more jolted if his hands had physically caressed her. She could feel the fiery blush that burned her skin as his gaze returned to her face.

'Dressing you has a great deal of appeal, I must admit,' he mused. Her gasp of outrage was met with a low chuckle. Closing his eyes again, as if in dismissal, he added, 'Wear blue. It's my favourite colour. Something sexy, with a neckline cut down to your knees. And your hair hanging loose. Just a little jewellery, maybe pearls, and for perfume I like a floral scent. . .'

She slammed the door behind her.

Hours later, Tracy felt confident that her appearance would make it quite clear to Neil Charles that she had no intention of catering to his demands. Her velvet gown, the colour of tree-ripening peaches, was strapless, with only the merest shadow of cleavage. A large matching taffeta bow secured her shoulder-length hair at the nape of the neck. Tracy hadn't needed Jess Baldwin's gasp of surprise to know that she glittered and sparkled like an over-decorated Christmas tree. A three-inch dog collar shimmered around her neck, and a multitude of bracelets twinkled on each arm, while the slightest movement of her head sent light bouncing off the opulent four-inch strands that dangled from her earlobes—the entire contents of Grandmother Nolan's jewellery chest. There was no need to announce that her grandfather had long ago replaced the real diamonds with fake. She took a deep breath. Sensuous, vanilla-scented perfume wafted upwards with each beat of her pulse.

Her presence this evening had nothing to do with Neil Charles's empty threats. After thinking the matter over in the quiet of Jess Baldwin's guest bedroom, Tracy had realised that restoring Stan's good name and catching the criminal were more important than her own feelings.

That was before she'd realised what an ordeal the party would be. Tracy could no longer pretend that she wasn't skulking back here in the corner, half-hidden by the silk monstrosity that Jess called a tree. Her first social occasion since the tragedy, and she should never have come. The three months that she'd been away hadn't been enough for the bad memories to fade. This evening had been proof of that: groups that drifted apart when she joined them, conversations that ceased at her arrival, and backs that turned ever so slightly in a casual but definite snub.

'Did you see who's here? Tracy Warner! A lot of people who own stock in Warner's company are here tonight. You'd think Jessica would have had more sense than to invite her.'

The woman's voice came from the other side of the tree, startling Tracy. She sank back against the wall.

'Those two have always been as thick as thieves, and Jess insists that what Stan Warner did had nothing to do with Tracy, since he wasn't her real father.'

'He wasn't?'

'Don't you remember? Maybe it was before you moved to Denver. Tracy's real father ran off with another woman, leaving Maureen, Tracy's mom, high and dry. It was almost as big a scandal as Stan Warner's crime and suicide. The Nolans, Maureen's family, were as top-drawer socially as the Warners.'

'Not any more.'

Tracy stood frozen with mortification as the two

women walked away, laughing with malicious enjoyment. At least they hadn't seen her. Loneliness washed over her. The piano player had switched from the rowdy honky-tonk he'd been belting out earlier to something sad and bluesy, and a few couples locked in each other's arms circled slowly around the floor of the nearby music room. From other rooms came the rising hum of conversation, punctuated with bursts of laughter. A beautiful arrangement of early spring flowers and forced flowering branches caught her eye. Red tulips. Her mother's favourite flowers. The back of her throat filled with tears, and she swallowed hard.

'Trace Warner as a wallflower? I'd never have guessed it.'

Tracy whirled around. Neil Charles was elegant in formal attire that accentuated his tall, trim body. In spite of the mocking words, the hazel eyes held a trace of compassion. He had overheard the catty remarks and dared to feel sorry for her. Her chin rose a notch. She had no intention of being anyone's object of pity. 'Perhaps you're not very good at guessing games, Mr Charles!' she snapped.

'Touchy this evening, aren't you? I suppose it's pretty tough discovering that you're no longer the belle of the ball.' His compassion was short-lived.

'Meaning, if I ever was, it was only because I was rich?'

He seemed to take in her appearance for the first time, and one corner of his mouth twitched. 'Good lord, why didn't you warn me to wear sunglasses? Well, never mind, I suppose I can always shut my eyes while we dance.'

Laughter was not the response she'd hoped to

elicit from him. 'I don't care to dance, Mr Charles,' she said coolly.

'Let me guess—the spoiled little rich girl isn't getting her own way, so she's going to be as obstructive as possible, never mind if her selfish and contemptible behaviour hampers clearing her stepfather's name? What did he ever do to you?' He grabbed her arm. 'Don't faint, damn you!'

His sharp voice reversed the flow of blood from her brain, and she could feel the hot colour burning her cheeks. 'I'm OK,' she said in a shaky voice which gave the lie to her words. His brutal accusation had been a knife-thrust to the heart. Because there was no denying the truth of what he'd said. For some reason this man penetrated her defences as no one had before and, because she resented that fact, she'd acted childishly, her desire to best him eclipsing her better self. Concentrating on his black bow-tie, she swallowed hard and forced herself to add, 'I deserved that. I *have* been behaving badly, and what's worse, I knew it, but I've been excusing it by pretending that it was all your fault.' Gathering her courage, she peeked up at him through her lashes. 'I-I'll co-operate from now on, Mr Charles.'

A peculiar expression settled on his face as he gazed down at her. 'The name is Neil, remember?'

'Neil,' she repeated obediently.

His brows drew together in a heavy frown.

'What?' she asked involuntarily, flinching as his fingers tightened their grip on her arm.

'You're a very dangerous woman, Tracy Warner,' he said softly, twin flames momentarily flaring deep within hazel eyes.

'I'm not. . .I don't know what. . .' She caught her

breath. 'You said earlier that no one thought that I had anything to do with. . .'

'I swear I do not think that you committed any crime.' His grip eased, his thumb trailing lazy cirlces on her arm. 'Unless that perfume you're wearing can be considered assault with a deadly weapon.'

'I thought you preferred floral scents.'

'Hate 'em,' he said promptly. 'I knew if I told you the truth, you'd run out and buy the biggest bottle of cheap carnation perfume that you could find.'

'You don't know me as well as you think you do,' she said, unnerved by his light, sensuous touch. A couple who used to play cards with her parents walked by. Tracy smiled and spoke to them, welcoming the interruption. They pretended that they didn't see her. A hot flush of embarrassment burned her cheeks.

'Let's dance,' Neil said harshly, his face cold and angry.

Tracy's spirits sank even further. The evening promised to be unendurable. Pretending to care for a man who disliked everything about her.

A steel arm around her waist gave her no choice in the matter, as Neil guided her towards the music-room. He leaned down, his breath warm against her cheek. 'And smile. Marie Antoinette looked happier headed for the guillotine!'

Once in the music-room they were the cynosure of all eyes. Tracy forced her mouth to curve in a travesty of a smile. For Marie Antoinette, the ordeal had been almost over. For Tracy, it was just beginning.

CHAPTER TWO

THE lights were dim in the music-room. Soft, dreamy love-songs flowed like thick chocolate syrup from the piano. Tracy moved into Neil's arms and wordlessly they moved around the room, her body somehow anticipating his every step. There were roses in this room, their heavy aroma a sensual contrast to the musky, masculine scent of Neil's cologne. He held her closely, the heat from his body encircling her, the only cool oasis the satin fabric of his dinner-jacket lapel against her left palm. Deep within Tracy, the oddest feeling that she'd found sanctuary began slowly to unfold, only to collide abruptly with a sense of longing as sharp and piercing as it was unfamiliar. She stumbled, to be immediately rescued by the strong arm around her waist. The music stopped with a light glissando of sharp, glittering notes that shattered her emotions like broken glass. She tried to step from Neil Charles's arms.

He allowed her only one step backwards. 'That wasn't so bad, was it?'

'I survived.'

'Smile when you say that, Pilgrim,' he said in a very bad John Wayne accent, a boyish grin lighting up his face. Tipping up her face with a single finger under her chin, he leaned down and whispered against her lips. 'We're being watched, and your performance so far isn't exactly up to Academy Award standards. You make an iceberg look warm.'

Swallowing the temptation to spit in one of those

hazel eyes that smiled with such false warmth, Tracy willed her body to soften and slightly lean in Neil's direction. Partially lowering her eyelids, she directed a flirtatious look up at him and slowly licked her bottom lip. 'Better?' she breathed.

'I'm not sure. I just remembered that the dangerous thing about icebergs is not how cold they are, but how much of them is hidden from view.' His eyes narrowed thoughtfully. 'How much of you is hidden from view? Finding out might prove interesting.'

Before she could decipher his cryptic remark, his head descended and his mouth pressed warmly against hers. The shock knocked her off balance and she swayed, only to catch herself by grabbing on to Neil's lapels. He tasted of wine. The voices of the other dancers faded away as Tracy clung to him. His hands slid down her back, and the heat from them penetrated her dress as he tugged her closer to him until the sensitive tips of her breasts pressed against his warm chest. His body heat seared her skin. Much as his lips seared her mouth.

The piano player finished a selection of rock music with a clanging clash of chords. Tracy wrenched her mouth from Neil's. He smiled lazily as a slow melody rippled from the piano, and pulled her tighter against his body, his thighs rubbing hers as he guided her about the dance-floor. 'Now I know how the *Titanic* felt,' he said in a wry voice.

Tracy tried to concentrate on the movements of the dance, but inwardly she was shaken by the chemistry that had exploded between them. Where was Tracy Warner's well-known cool sophistication when she needed it? It had served successfully as her armour against fortune-hunters and social climbers from the first moment she'd realised the difficulties in distinguishing between admiration for her and admiration for her purse and social background. Neil Charles, who couldn't make clearer his disdain for rich, young, society ladies, had penetrated her shield with dangerous ease. And not because he was likeable or friendly or exerting himself the least little bit to please. On the contrary, he went out of his way to be rude, arrogant and insensitive. She admitted his physical attraction, and he was obviously very experienced in the art of pleasing ladies. But she was one lady who had no intention of being pleased. And the best way to discourage any ideas he might have was to remind him how much he disliked her type. Flashing him a bogus smile, she said, 'You're no slouch in the acting department yourself. Your performance of a man smitten by my charms is masterly.'

'What makes you think it's an act? A beautiful strawberry-blonde with eyes that appear cold as grey steel, until one gets close enough to see they're really blue with white flecks. Soft, creamy shoulders that beg for a man's lips, not to mention a mouth with a full bottom lip that cries out to be nibbled on. And did I mention a body. . .'

Tracy nodded in approval. 'That's very good.' She thrust aside a flicker of pleasure. The man was merely pretending.

His eyes glinted down at her. 'Praise indeed from a woman who acts as superbly as you do. Your kiss was very convincing.'

'I couldn't have you casting aspersions on my abilities. I was taught to act practically from the cradle. Along with ballroom dancing, proper dress, party planning, how to hire a cook, which decorator to use, which wine to serve——'

Fortunately he interrupted her before she ran out of ideas. 'I wasn't aware that the theatrical world rated so highly on your social scale.'

Tracy uttered a high, artificial laugh and gave his cheek a condescending pat. 'Of course it does. Young ladies in my social echelon have to know how to act, in order to disguise their real feelings behind sociably acceptable behaviour. As my Grandmother Nolan used to say, we do not show our petticoats in public, nor do we wash our dirty laundry there.'

He frowned down at her. 'A million-dollar education, and all you can do is talk in clichés.'

She smiled graciously. 'The wonderful thing about clichés is that they are so apt. Life is much easier when one has rules to live by.'

The music ended and Neil whirled her into the nearest corner, studying her face as if she belonged to a foreign species. 'Jake said his daughter used to be a warm and generous girl, who lavishly bestowed her heart on those she loved,' he said in a slow, deliberate voice. 'I suppose all that was trained right out of you.'

Tracy froze. The last thing she wanted was Neil Charles coming into her home and attempting to psychoanalyse her. The pianist switched to a livelier tune. Pasting a smile on her face, she looked up at Neil. 'Shouldn't we dance again? Just in case people are watching?'

Neil guided her from the corner and then stepped away, his body moving lazily to the heavy, throbbing beat. They seldom touched, but the air between them was charged with an electric tension that seemed to snap and sparkle as they danced. There was a burst of applause as the pianist ended the song with a triumphant flourish. Tracy was flushed, her heart pounding.

'This may be the most interesting assignment I've had,' Neil said, a look of speculation on his face.

Blake Campbell spared Tracy the need to answer. 'Tracy, love. Welcome back. Jess told me that you'd be here tonight.'

'I'm not your love,' Tracy automatically denied as she greeted her stepfather's plant manager.

A drink held in one hand, Blake gave her a crooked smile before looking enquiringly at Neil. Tracy introduced the men to each other.

Blake appraised Neil curiously. 'Neil Charles? You must be a newcomer to Denver.'

'My first visit,' Neil answered.

Blake dismissed him, turning back to Tracy, his face grave. 'I couldn't help but notice the way some of these people are treating you like Typhoid Mary.' His voice deepened with contempt as he looked around the room. 'They're fools. Anyone who knows you should be well aware that you had nothing to do with the mess.'

Tracy was touched by his brusque partisanship. 'Thank you.'

'If there's anything I can do. . .'

'It's kind of you to offer, but Tracy is my responsibility,' Neil said smoothly, pulling her closer to his side in an unmistakable gesture of possession.

Blake's face immediately registered the significance of Neil's actions. Tracy could almost see the thoughts rearranging themselves in Blake's mind until they had shifted into this new alignment. Fair-haired with blue-eyed good looks, and always perfectly attired, Blake's perpetual air of bored arrogance was viewed as a challenge by most women, but Tracy had been content with their casual friendship. The quick flash she'd seen in his eyes must have been one of surprise. It couldn't have been jealousy. She studied him from beneath lowered lashes until the context of Neil's words hit her. He was explaining how they'd met the previous Christmas at Vail. How did he know she'd been there with her parents? She felt his arm tighten about her waist at her quick start of surprise.

'I'm glad that Tracy has someone to help her during this difficult time,' Blake said. 'But my offer to help still stands. Stan did a lot of work at home. Now, don't take this wrong, Charles, but his paperwork would be incomprehensible to an outsider, and someone like you could make a real mess of things.'

'That's very thoughtful of you to offer to help,' Tracy said hastily as Neil stiffened at her side. 'But I think that the police and lawyers took care of all that.' Quickly she changed the subject. A few pleasantries were exchanged, and then Blake drifted away.

'Campbell an old boyfriend?' Neil asked, watching the other man's departure.

'No. He worked for my stepfather.' Her back was warm where Neil's hand still rested on her waist.

'Strange. I could have sworn I detected a tinge of animosity in his attitude. It seemed to me that he couldn't quite believe you'd pick someone like me over him?'

'Well,' Tracy said tartly, 'I didn't, did I? Besides, Blake's all right,' she defended him. 'He might come across as conceited, but I think that's a defence mechanism to cover an inferiority complex. Stan mentioned something once about a poor childhood. I know that Stan was fond of him.'

'Why wasn't he an old boyfriend? He's got all the right credentials. Snappy dresser, not bad looking, good job.'

'You forgot to add that he drives a foreign sports car. I refuse to date any man who drives a sedan.'

Neil laughed before adding drily, 'I suppose that his social background didn't quite measure up.'

'How astute of you,' Tracy marvelled, determined not to let his needling upset her. 'I was terrified he'd use the wrong fork at the dinner-table. Breeding always tells, you know. I have to think of my children.'

'Planning to have many?'

'Two, I think.'

'You wouldn't want to overburden the nanny.'

'Exactly.' Peering up from under her thick lashes, she gave him a brilliantly smug smile before cooing, 'Kindness to the lower orders is so important, don't you think?'

'What I think is that, if you look at me like that once more, I'm going to kiss you.'

'Good.' Tracy refused to be disconcerted. 'I did enjoy the last one. Although, perhaps a little more feeling if you want to convince everyone here that we're "an item".' Swallowing an insane urge to giggle at the stunned look on his face, she went on, 'Your story about our meeting on the ski slopes was quick thinking. I suppose you read that in the papers, too. We'll have to enlarge upon it. A girl like me might pick up a stranger for a few laughs, but I'd never have the bad taste to introduce him to my friends in Denver unless he was socially acceptable.' He needn't know she'd never picked up a man in her life. 'Good looks are not enough in my crowd. Let's see,' she mused, 'what occupation can we give you?'

'A schoolteacher,' he suggested, leading her back to the dance-floor.

'Please!' Tracy said, a pained expression on her face.

'Politician?'

She grimaced.

'Artist?'

'Too bohemian.'

'Lawyer on Wall Street?'

Tracy wrinkled up her nose. 'Boring, but acceptable.' A sudden thought made her laugh. 'Can you imagine the reaction if I suddenly announced to everyone that you're a private detective sent by my father to be my bodyguard? It must be positively in the worst taste to dance with one's bodyguard.'

Neil's eyes narrowed. 'Where did you get the idea that I'm a private detective?'

'I assumed it. You're supposed to protect me—what else?'

'I'm a lawyer in Jake's firm. I'm doing this as a special favour for him.'

Tracy stopped dead on the dance-floor. 'You work with my. . .with him?'

He guided her back into step with the music. 'Does it make a difference?'

'I guess not.' Private detective or lawyer, in either case Neil was employed by her father and carrying out his orders. It was only a matter of a few weeks, and then he would head back east and she could repair the tattered fabric of her life without any reminders of her past. Neil Charles was nothing more than a minor inconvenience, a man who, having arrived with a preconceived notion of her, didn't like her. . .Neil's dislike of her was suddenly personalised. It wasn't that he didn't like her type; he didn't like *her*. Influenced by her father.

Tracy wasn't sure how she got through the rest of the evening. Certainly Neil had no reason to question her acting abilities. She smiled shyly into his eyes, touched him at every opportunity, and introduced him with loving pride to all those whose curiosity exceeded their wariness. Of course, there were loyal friends who had stuck by her following the tragedy, and they were so obviously pleased for her that she regretted the need to deceive them, but Neil insisted that there were to be no exceptions. Only Ed and Jess Baldwin were aware of the true circumstances surrounding Neil's presence. Keeping up the pretence was exhausting, the evening endless. By the time all of the Baldwins' guests had departed, Tracy was only too happy to bid Neil a quick goodnight.

The next morning she emerged slowly from the welcome oblivion of sleep, fighting consciousness, dreading that first moment of awareness. Sleep, ever fickle, refused to give her sanctuary, and Tracy opened her eyes reluctantly. Heavy taffeta curtains draped the windows and shrouded the enormous four-poster bed, giving Jesse's luxurious guest bedroom the darkened appeal of a tomb. An overwhelming despondency pressed Tracy deep against a smothering pile of smooth, linen-covered pillows while painful memories washed over her.

Three and a half months ago she'd been quietly content with her life. How quickly one's life could be turned topsy-turvy. A fact that no one should know better than she. A rich, spoiled brat, Neil had called her. What did he know of true riches? First she'd lost her father, then her grandparents, then. . .Her stomach contracted painfully. After seeing Stan and her mother lying there. . .nothing that happened to her in the future could ever be that horrible. No matter what she thought of Jake Archer, she had to believe that he would prove Stan's innocence.

Jake Archer. How ironic that the man whom Maureen had hated with such passion was going to inherit everything she'd owned, while her only child received nothing. Tracy wouldn't care, except for her home. The one constant in her life. Everyone she had ever loved had left her, but the house had always been there. 'I *can* put up with his mockery, his sneering remarks. I *can*!' she proclaimed out loud to the empty room.

Several hours later Tracy had reason to question her rash declaration. From the moment that Neil Charles had greeted the sight of her van with raised eyebrows, he had treated her with an air of cool mockery that had her longing to claw his eyes out. Biting back an angry retort, she gave the steering-wheel a vicious jerk, turning into the exclusive Denver neighbourhood where her parents had lived. The guard at the gate saluted her familiar van with a friendly wave.

A whistle escaped Neil's pursed lips, his eyebrows shooting up to his hairline. 'Be it ever so humble. No wonder you threw a tantrum at the thought of losing it. I didn't realise we were talking about the Taj Mahal.'

Tracy concentrated on parking the van squarely in front of the immense double doors that faced the circle driveway, before turning off the engine. 'This isn't my house.' Reluctantly she reached for her key-ring.

'I know. It's Jake's.'

She welcomed the note of irony in his voice. Anger at him would distract her thoughts and keep the unspeakable memories at bay. 'You didn't do your homework,' she said, stepping down from the van. 'My grandmother's house is in Palmer Lake, south of Denver. This is Stan's house. He left it to his sister.'

'The one in Ireland?' Neil trailed her to the front door. 'Is that why you immediately flew over there after the funeral? To convince her to give it back to you?'

Naturally, he *would* think that. 'Why else? Stan left her everything.' She savagely jabbed the key in the front door lock.

Inside the house, the air was stale and warm. A faint odour of cleanser stung Tracy's nostrils as she trod the familiar black and white marble squares. While she'd been in Europe the blood and police marks had been cleaned off the carpeting, so Tracy knew that the house held no visible clues to the horrible tragedy that had occurred there, but the ghastly chalk outlines would forever haunt her memories.

'This where it happened?' Neil stood under the large arch looking into the living-room.

'Yes.'

Her voice must have betrayed her because he gave her a quick, assessing look. 'First time you've been here since it happened?'

'Yes. No. I was here right after the. . .afterwards.' She took a deep breath. 'Look around if you want. I have to pick up a couple of things.' Refusing to look into the living-room, she bolted up the Persian-clad staircase to her parents' suite.

Her mother had called several days before the tragedy to tell her that she had boxed up a number of Tracy's possessions for her to pick up. Tracy had intended to come by on the day of the tragedy, but she'd been so engrossed in her work that the errand had totally slipped her mind. Maybe if she had come. . .Firmly she shoved the thought away. Such speculating wouldn't help.

Her mother's dressing-room. Maureen Warner might have stepped out for only a moment. The closet door was partially open, a frilly négligé in her mother's favourite shade of green hanging in front. High-heeled slippers, trimmed with feathers, lay sideways on the floor. In front of an ornate mirror, crystal bottles and silver-lidded jars glittered on the marble-topped dressing-table. Tracy sat down on the dressing-table bench, then slowly picked up the flacon of her mother's favourite perfume and dabbed some on her neck. The familiar scent brought on an onrush of memories, and hot tears stung the inside of Tracy's eyelids as she held the perfume stopper beneath her nose, sniffing deeply. But it wasn't possible to conjure back the past. It never had been.

'Hardly a hand-to-mouth existence.' Neil stood in the doorway, looking threateningly masculine in the frivolous, feminine abode.

His jeering remark dried the gathering tears, and she whipped up her anger against him. 'Spying on me? Now that you know everything in here belongs either to Jake Archer or Aunt Sally, I suppose you're following me around to make sure that I don't steal anything.'

Neil stiffened. 'I'm sure that Jake would want you to have your mother's clothes and stuff.' He gestured vaguely around the rom.

'No,' Tracy said sharply. 'They belong to him. I want nothing of his.' She put the stopper back in the bottle and set it down with shaking fingers. 'I came for my things. My mother called me to say. . .before. . .they should be in boxes with my name on them in the back of her closet.'

Neil brushed her aside as she stood up. 'I'll get them. I came up to tell you that you've got company. Blake Campbell.'

'Blake? Why is he here?'

'He mumbled something about papers and headed for the back of the house,' Neil explained, disappearing into the closet.

Tracy found Blake in her stepfather's office, rummaging through his desk. 'What are you looking for?'

'Nothing in particular. I just thought there might be some papers from the business here.' A hand on her back, he guided her from the room. 'I couldn't believe it when Jessica told me that you'd come over here. Why put yourself through this ordeal when I told you I'd help? You should have called me,' he chided.

'I was just picking up some boxes my mother called me about before. . .'

'I'll do that. You go wait in your car. It's bad enough that the police made you come over here that day.'

Tracy shook off the insistent hand propelling her through the foyer. 'They needed me to identify th-them, and to see if anything was missing. Mother's jewels, that sort of thing.'

'They should have located the housekeeper, even if it was her day off.'

'Mrs Chambers would have had hysterics all over the house, which wouldn't have been of the slightest use to the police. Besides, they were my parents. The least I could do for them was to give the police any aid they asked for. I admit that it—it was awful, but

I'd never forgive myself if I allowed a—a little queasiness to stand in my way.'

'Nonsense. Maureen and Stan would have been appalled.'

'They would have expected me to do what needed to be done.'

'I think I have them all.' Neil stood half-way down the staircase, several boxes teetering precariously in his arms. Light streaming through the high, arched window on the landing behind him surrounded him with a golden aura.

His arrival appeared to be the signal for Blake to leave, and soon Tracy's van was headed south. Neil, having won the battle of who would drive, was behind the wheel.

'I'm perfectly capable of driving my own car,' Tracy said.

'Of course you are,' Neil agreed. 'I just thought that you looked a little tired today.'

'Thank you very much,' Tracy retorted. 'I'm an ungrateful daughter, a spoiled brat, a cry-baby, a weakling, and now an old hag. You certainly are hard on the ego.' She stared out of the window. The late April afternoon was mild, and a visitor to Colorado might have supposed that spring was firmly entrenched. Tracy was too well-versed in the vagaries of the weather along the Front Range to be similarly fooled.

Neil skilfully guided the van through a cluster of slow-moving cars. 'Don't make the mistake of confusing me with Campbell. He's the one who thinks you ought to be wrapped in cotton. For my money, you're a pretty tough broad.'

'Pretty tough broad?' Tracy echoed, turning to look at him.

He took his eyes from the road long enough to grin at her. 'It's a compliment. You were a real class act last night.'

Tracy arched one brow in disbelief. 'Kind words from you? I'm overwhelmed.'

'Don't get me wrong. I still think that you're part of the selfish, spoiled, idle rich, but you've got guts. The way some of those so-called friends of yours treated you last night, I would have expected you to run away at the first opportunity, but you stuck it out to the bitter end.'

Tracy's initial reaction was anger. How dared he judge her before he knew her? Then the realisation struck her that he was as surprised at his praise of her as she was. Neil had firmly placed her in a narrow category in his mind, and her refusal to stay there disconcerted him.

On an impulse, she said, 'I suppose if I admitted that I'd wanted to run last night, you'd think that I was a coward.'

'No. You didn't, that's what counts.' He hesitated. 'I had no idea it would be like that when I forced your hand about attending.'

'And if you had, you would have let me stay away?'

He shook his head slowly. 'No. We had to go. It was the best way to broadcast that you're no longer living alone, and at the same time give a plausible explanation for my presence.'

There was a long silence in the van as the miles sped past. Large patches of dingy, unmelted snow, left-overs from last week's spring storm, decorated the dormant landscape. They had left the road behind before Tracy finally spoke her thoughts out loud.

'There are times that you almost convince me.' In response to his inquisitive look, she added, 'That I might really be in danger.'

Neil shrugged. 'Jake seemed to think so.'

'Why didn't he ask the police to protect me?'

'On what grounds? He didn't have enough proof. Intuition doesn't get you very far with police.'

'Then why not ask Ed Baldwin to keep an eye on me?'

'He did for the few days between your return from Ireland and my arrival, but Ed's a busy man. At best, any eye he kept on you would be a cursory one. Jake wanted someone who would stick to you like glue.'

'Such as you.'

'Such as me,' he confirmed.

'Blake would have stayed with me.'

'I don't doubt that. He couldn't have made it plainer that he resented my existence.'

'You keep implying that there is something between Blake and me, but you couldn't be more wrong.' A look of scepticism crossed his face at her disclaimer and she added hastily, 'And before you make any more nasty cracks about his society credentials, let me assure you that Blake was no more interested in establishing any kind of relationship than I was. I admit he took me out a couple of times, but frankly, I think that my money and social status appealed to him more than I did.'

'Do I detect a hint of pique?' Neil asked, slowing down for a sharp curve.

'No matter what you think, I prefer that a person looks at me with all my faults and imperfections than at my cheque-book or my ancestors,' Tracy retorted. A red-winged blackbird, sitting on the fence, took to the air as they passed, his scarlet shoulder-patches flashing aggressively in the afternoon sun.

Neil ignored her challenge. 'If you're correct about Campbell, then it's surprising that he dropped you. The boss's daughter and all. . .' His voice trailed off suggestively.

'Stepdaughter.'

Neil gave her a puzzled look. 'What's the difference?'

Fortunately, driving reclaimed his attention as the van bumped across some railroad tracks, sparing Tracy the need to answer. Through the open window came the squeals of small children playing near the lake in the small park. Happy children, with fathers who loved them. Stan Warner had been crazy about Tracy's mother, and he'd accepted Tracy in much the same way he'd accepted Maureen's rugs and furniture. Mentally, Tracy shook herself free of self-pity. Stan had always treated her kindly and fairly. It wasn't his fault that he couldn't love another man's daughter, no matter how much that small girl had needed his love.

Neil broke into her reflections. 'Is Palmer Lake an old farming town?'

Ahead of them the small community sprawled over the hillside. 'Not really. While it's true that at one time this area was noted for its potato farms, the town itself was designed as a summer resort by officials from the Denver and Rio Grande Railroad Company back in the 1880s. Today it's mostly a bedroom community for Denver and Colorado Springs.' As she directed Neil through the town they passed houses whose ages spanned the century, houses of all shapes and sizes, running haphazardly down the hill towards the small lake. 'Here we are.' She pointed to an old house clinging to the hillside.

'This is it?' he asked in surprise.

'Yes.' As she jumped down from the high seat she was greeted by the fragrant scent of damp pine. Walking around to the back of the van, she looked to the east where a huge red rock with an oddly shaped arch resembled a giant elephant.

'Quite a view,' Neil said as he stood beside her.

Tracy nodded. Far to the south lay the sprawling environs of Colorado Springs, and off to the east were the dark hills of the Black Forest and the vast reaches of the eastern plains. She sighed with contentment. Home. She'd been away too long. Snatching up a couple of her bags, she led the way up the porch stairs, her pace quickening with each step.

The entrance hall, a page from yesteryear with its dark mahogany wainscoting, welcomed them inside. Dropping her luggage, Tracy flipped a switch, turning on the brass light fixture with its etched rose-glass globes, and looked around possessively at the creamy, papered walls sprigged with blue and rose.

Neil set a large box on the faded rose-coloured Chinese floral rug, his gaze sweeping the hall before coming back to rest on her face. 'This is it?' he repeated. 'The house you don't want your father to have?'

Tracy nodded. 'My maternal grandparents bought it back in the forties for their summer house. It was originally built around the turn of the century by some rich Texans who came up for chautauqua. I can't imagine lovelier surroundings for spending the summer in religious and educational pursuits, but Grandmother said that Jake Archer hated it here. He was bored.' She moved into the old-fashioned front parlour. Big, slouchy, rose-coloured upholstered pieces and massive dark furniture rested with calm assurance on the huge cabbage-roses of the faded burgundy rug. Walking around the room, she opened the heavy curtains, allowing in the late afternoon sun to dissipate an air of abandoned gloom.

Neil followed her into the room. 'I'm curious. Why didn't your grandmother leave the house to you?'

'You still think I'm interested in the money, don't you?' Tracy said slowly. 'I'd be wasting my time trying to explain.'

'Try me,' he invited.

Tracy smoothed a crocheted doily on the back of a chair. 'Grandmother and I spent a lot of time down here after Grandfather Nolan died.' She glanced at Neil. He was studying the collection of turquoise and deep pink pottery that filled the corner cupboard. 'Grandfather lost most of his money on bad investments. When he died, Grandmother had to sell the house in Denver to pay off his debts. If it hadn't been for Stan. . .he was so good to her. She told me once that the only thing she had to leave her daughter, my mother, was this house. It wasn't that Mother wanted this house—she preferred Stan's condo in Vail—but she would have been so hurt if Grandmother had passed her over. I understood. It was really just a technicality, because some day the house would be mine. We thought,' she added bitterly. 'I borrowed money from Stan and upgraded the windows and the insulation so that I could live here year-around. That the house might. . .you know. . .never occurred to me.' She walked back out into the hall.

'You borrowed?' Neil was right behind her. 'Is that another way of saying Warner gave you the money?'

Tracy gave him a cool stare. 'Certainly he gave it to me. At current interest rates. Stan knew that I wouldn't want to be beholden to him; the loan was purely business. I paid back every cent and we celebrated by burning the papers in my fireplace.' At the memory a smile flickered across her face, quickly replaced by a scowl as she recalled that it wasn't her fireplace now.

Neil uttered a short laugh. 'I can tell the instant your thoughts turn to your father. A big black thundercloud covers your face.'

CHAPTER THREE

'Is THAT so surprising?' Tracy bent to pick up her bags. 'Considering his threat to take my home away from me.' Half-way up the wooden staircase, she turned around. 'There are only two bedrooms upstairs. The small one is the guest room. I'm afraid we'll have to share the bathroom.'

'One bathroom?'

There was an odd note in Neil's voice, which immediately put Tracy on the defensive. 'If you don't like the accommodation, you don't have to stay.'

'Good try, but even if we have to share a bed and go outside to a privy I'm here for the duration. And don't you forget it.'

As if she could, she thought resentfully, unpacking her suitcases. The house which had once seemed so cosy now felt cramped with Neil's incessant whistling and ringing footsteps. An alien interloper invading her territory. Only it wasn't her territory. No matter how much or how often she railed against the circumstances, no matter what her grandmother had promised, no matter what her mother had intended, there was no changing the results. Because of her mother's long-forgotten will, this house now belonged to Jake Archer.

Perhaps she should just thumb her nose at Jake Archer and move out. Wearily she sank down on the bed to consider her plight. It was stupid to give a house such importance. A bunch of boards, that was all it was. She should give up, find a small place to rent. A heavy feeling of depression settled over her at the thought of moving to a sterile apartment. This house suited her. More than that, the house, over eighty years old, represented stability and sanctuary. Even as a child she'd always had the fanciful notion that the house welcomed her. Determination stiffened her spine and she rose to her feet, sweeping up a pile of dresses to hang in the closet. Jake Archer was not going to drive her from her home. Footsteps bounded down the staircase. Nor was his representative.

Neil was in the kitchen when she finally went downstairs. 'I made some sandwiches,' he said over his shoulder.

Tracy looked at the bread and cold cuts spread over the counter-top, and an embarrassed flush coloured her cheeks. She'd completely forgotten her intention to stop at a grocery store on her way down. 'Where did you get the food?'

'Have you heard of a recent development called a grocery store?'

'Of course I have, but. . .'

'But you've never been in one. It figures.'

The man was determined to label her one of nature's drones. She had no intention of disillusioning him. If he wanted a rich, spoiled brat. . .Wincing in exaggeration at her hands, she said, 'Darn. A chipped nail. *You* should have carried in my luggage.'

'I'm your bodyguard, not a servant.' His voice was frigid.

Tracy widened her eyes at him. 'As long as you're here, you may as well be useful. Surely it's obvious that, with you in the extra bedroom, there's no room for a maid?' There was no need for him to know that she'd been doing her own cleaning ever since she'd moved to Palmer Lake.

'I see. And I suppose you expect me to do the cooking.'

'Cooking?' she asked with a sinking feeling. Neil looked as if he enjoyed a good meal, and her bank account was in no condition to support such enjoyment. Why hadn't she thought to borrow some money from Jess or Ed? She could imagine Neil's scornful reaction if she admitted that she could barely afford to feed herself, much less a big hunk like him.

'Let me guess.' He gave an exaggerated sigh. 'You don't know how to cook.'

She eyed him limpidly as she pulled out a kitchen chair and sat down. 'Just one of those things I never learned at my mother's knee.' Not exactly a lie. Lessons from Stan's housekeeper could hardly be called learning at her mother's knee.

'Fortunately, I did.' He sliced a sandwich and slid the plate towards her. 'I only picked up a couple of things this morning.' Joining her at the large, scrubbed pine table, he pulled a small notepad and a pen from his pocket. 'I'll have to shop again tomorrow. What do you like to eat?'

Tracy shrugged. 'Simple food. Lobster, prime rib, fillet, some caviare for a light snack. . .'

'Never mind.' He put away the pad. 'I'll plan the menus. I'm sure this is a stupid question, but do you need cleaing supplies?'

'Whatever for?'

'Cleaning toilets, mopping floors, little things like that,' he said, his voice heavily coated with sarcasm.

'Surely you don't expect me. . .' she asked in horror.

Neil studied her for a very long moment before

speaking. 'I think we need a few ground rules. I happen to like to eat, so I'll do the grocery shopping and cook the meals, yours included—not because I'm your servant, but simply because it's no more trouble to cook for two than one. I'm not a nut about cleanliness, but I do like to live in a reasonably dirt-free environment, so I'll do my share to maintain one and I'll expect the same from you, especially since we have to share the bathroom. I can't tolerate hair clogging the drains or toothpaste spilled in the sink.'

'Ah, a man of standards,' she mocked, draining her coffee-cup. 'Aren't you afraid that exposure to someone like me might sully your lily-white character?'

'Maybe the reverse will be true. Maybe a little of me will rub off on you.'

'I hope not,' Tracy said instantly. 'I'd hate to become bigoted, close-minded, arrogant, insulting, superior, rude, overbearing, hard-hearted and—all the other things you are.'

To Tracy's surprise, Neil laughed. 'You're Jake's kid all right. Same temper. Same tendency to go for the other man's throat when your own position is weak.'

Tracy stiffened. 'If you intend to live in my house, you will not compare me to. . .to. . .that. . .*him*!' As he opened his mouth an outflung hand forestalled his anticipated response. 'I know. *His* house.' Her chair scraped loudly against the old linoleum floor as she pushed it back and stood up.

'I wasn't going to say that,' Neil objected. 'I just wondered why you never visited your father after the divorce.'

'Why should I? He left me. If he wanted to see me,

he knew where I lived.' She snatched her dirty dishes from the table.

'Maybe it wasn't that simple for him.'

'Why not? Was he in jail? Crippled? Or was it just that she wouldn't let him?' Standing at the sink, Tracy turned on the water faucet with an angry twist.

'You mean your mother?'

'No. The woman he married.' She dumped soap in the sink and then abruptly turned to gather up the remainder of the dishes. The sudden movement sent her crashing into Neil, who was headed towards the sink with his dirty dishes. Taken by surprise, Tracy clutched at his arm, struggling to regain her balance.

A strong arm encircled her waist, steadying her on her feet. 'Are you all right?'

The warmth from his body crept over hers, stealing the strength from traitorous muscles which longed to lean on someone stronger, if only for an instant. Through sheer will-power alone, Tracy forced her body to break the contact. 'Yes, I—I'm fine. Thank you, I'm sorry, I. . .' The words died away as she looked up into Neil's face looming over her, a strange emotion darkening his hazel eyes.

'I'm not the least bit sorry,' he said. 'It isn't every day that a beautiful woman throws herself at me.' His head lowered.

'No.' She jerked her head away. 'I didn't. Don't.'

He laughed softly. 'You said my kisses need practice.'

'I've changed my mind.'

'Too bad.'

The mocking words were spoken against her closed lips as he brought his mouth down upon hers. He tasted of coffee. His hands gripped her shoulders, one thumb inscribing slow circles on the side of her neck, the other pressing lightly on the pulse that beat wildly at the base of her throat. Penned between the sink cabinet and his hard frame, she could feel the heat emanating from his body. The tap was still turned on, the loud, rushing sound drowning out the rapid drumbeat of her heart, while soapy, lemon-scented steam rose up to curl around her nose. Suddenly, deep within her, his kiss dynamited the rigid restraints she'd kept on her tormented emotions. A compelling need to be held and comforted exploded to the surface. Desperately she clung to him, her fingers digging deep into his shoulder muscles, her body pressing fiercely against his.

Neil dragged his mouth from hers. 'You're full of surprises, aren't you? First you do the dishes, and then this.'

Tracy opened her eyes. The dispassionate appraisal in the gaze which met hers sent shock surging throughout her body. How could she have kissed him like that? Her emotions boiled and churned into a treacherous whirlpool which threatened to drown her in its chaotic centre. A loud gurgling sound assaulted her ears as dampness chilled her skin. Then Neil pushed her away, and she watched helplessly as water cascaded from the flooded sink. Dropping to his knees, he began to wipe the floor with a kitchen towel. There was a mop at the top of the stairs, but she was incapable of telling him so.

Wringing out the towel over the draining sink, Neil gave her a cool glance. 'Sorry about your blouse. I should know better than to interrupt a dishwasher at work.'

'What?' She finally found her voice.

'Your blouse. It's sopping.'

'Oh.' No wonder she was cold. More than cold.

Chilled all the way through. Her mind could barely grasp what Neil was saying. Shame and contempt for her behaviour flooded through her. The sensation of fabric sliding over her shoulders jerked her from her trance. 'What are you doing?' Fear drove the blood from her face and she clutched the blouse closed over her breast.

'I'm not accepting your very obvious invitation, if that's what you mean,' Neil said impatiently. 'I was simply helping you off with your blouse. It's soaking wet and you're shivering.'

Tracy's mind stuck on the word 'invitation'. Numbly she shook her head, wanting to deny his conclusions, but not blaming him for reaching them. The way she'd behaved. . .impossible to explain to him her sudden conviction that his arms offered her sanctuary from the outside world. Was she so desperate for solace that she would seek it from this man whose low opinion of her was conveyed with his every word? Unable to face him, she turned her back to him. 'Just go away,' she said in a tight voice that seemed unconnected to a body that was alternately cold with horror and hot with shame.

Neil walked from the room without saying a word.

Tracy sagged against the kitchen-table, her shaking legs offering little support. She couldn't stop trembling; her body was chilled inside the damp clothing. Falling into the nearest chair, her head dropped on to arms crossed on the table. She was so tired, so weary. The tears she'd fought off for months were no longer to be denied.

She was still sitting at the table, loud, wrenching sobs convulsively shaking her body, when a strong arm encircled her waist and lifted her from the chair. A warm blanket was dropped over her shoulders and she huddled thankfully within its depths. When her tears finally lessened and the shudders died away Tracy found herself on the living-room sofa, Neil's arms wrapped around her while he patted her awkwardly on the shoulder. Tugging the blanket more securely in place, she edged away from him. He pulled her back, at the same time managing to extract a handkerchief from his pocket. She took it without a word and noisily blew her nose.

'So much for you being a pretty tough broad.'

The amusement in his voice was not lost on her. 'I'm sure you're thrilled to have your theory that I'm a spoiled cry-baby confirmed,' she said, her voice still clogged with tears.

He brushed aside a wisp of hair that clung damply to her forehead. 'I knew you'd hold it against me that your tears yesterday didn't work.'

She jerked her head away from his touch. 'You are the most arrogant. . .my crying had nothing to do with you!' Angrily she dashed a tear from her face.

'I'm aware of that. You were feeling sorry for yourself.'

'So what if I was?' Defiantly she blew her nose again. 'I'm not the first person who cried when her parents died.' Finding a clean spot on the hanky, she wiped the dampness from her face, ignoring the fact that most of her tears had been soaked up by his shirt-front.

The arm about her shoulders tightened. 'If you cared so much about them, you wouldn't have been so ready to believe that Stan was guilty,' he said.

Tracy wiggled from beneath his arm and stood up clutching the blanket around her. 'I don't have to stay here and listen to your stupid remarks. You have no idea what I believed or why.'

Taking hold of the blanket's edges, Neil yanked her back down on the sofa beside him. 'Then suppose you convince me I'm wrong.'

'Why should I bother?'

'The sooner this mess is cleared up, the sooner I'm gone.'

It couldn't be too soon for her. 'I never believed that Stan embezzled that money or murdered my mother. I—I thought,' she stumbled over the words, reluctant to voice her theory out loud, 'that my mother committed suicide, and when Stan found her he couldn't bear life without her and turned the gun on himself.'

Neil frowned down at her, his brows knit in puzzlement. 'Where did you come up with that crazy idea?'

'It's not so crazy,' Tracy insisted. 'My mother was beautiful, but she was also very insecure. Living with a man like Jake Archer didn't help, especially the way he abandoned her when I was eight. Fortunately, Stan was right there to pick up the pieces, but Mother was convinced that he only loved her because she was beautiful, and she was terrified that when she grew old and ugly he'd leave her, too.'

'And you think that a wrinkle or a grey hair drove her to suicide?' Neil asked in disgust.

Tracy took a deep breath, forcing herself to ignore Neil's disparaging remark. 'Mother was convinced that she had Alzheimer's disease. Things started to confuse her. She was forgetting appointments, dinner engagements, where she'd put her reading-glasses. Stan and I begged her to go to the doctor, but she refused.' She folded the handkerchief into little squares on her lap. 'Stan adored my mother from their first meeting as children and he'd always hoped to marry her, but Jake Archer came along and stole her away. Their divorce was his second chance. Mother was wrong about Stan. He would never have left her.'

'Why didn't you say something to the police?'

'I did, but when the audit at the office disclosed that money was missing they were so sure that Stan had panicked and killed them both that they wouldn't listen to me. The lieutenant pointed out that I had no proof that Mother had committed suicide. The prints on the gun were smudged and the only ones they could read were Stan's.' Tracy wiped a tear from her cheek. 'The ironic part is that the coroner's autopsy established that Mother didn't have Alzheimer's. A few weeks before she died she was struck on the head by a falling flowerpot in the greenhouse. She seemed OK, but apparently the blow caused blood clots which were pressing against her brain. If she'd gone to the doctor, X-rays would have disclosed the damage and an operation to drain the clots would have taken care of her problem.' Tracy barely noticed that her tears were flowing again. 'You were right in accusing me of being selfish. If only I hadn't been so busy with my own concerns, if only I had forced her to go to the doctor——'

'Stop it,' Neil ordered. Taking back his sodden handkerchief, he handed her a paper tissue from the box on the table beside them. 'Donning a hair shirt won't change anything.'

'You don't have a sympathetic bone in your body, do you?' Tracy asked bitterly.

'Sympathy? Is that what you want? I thought you wanted Stan's name cleared and the mystery solved. Hell, sympathy is easy. I'll just put my arms around you and croon "poor baby" a couple of times, and that will make everything OK, won't it?'

'Damn you!' Tracy cried. 'You love to put me in the wrong, don't you?'

'You do that all by yourself, Tracy, all by yourself.'

Tracy jumped to her feet, leaving the crumpled blanket clutched in Neil's grasp. 'You're the meanest, most hateful person I've ever met. I loathe you.'

Neil uttered a harsh laugh. 'Good. Then you won't mind if I insist on a hands-off policy with regard to each other.'

'Mind?' Tracy screeched, turning in the doorway to stare incredulously at him. 'You're crazy if you think I'd want anything else.'

'Am I?' he asked, an odd inflection in his voice. 'Out in the kitchen——'

'Forget out in the kitchen!' she raged.

Neil shrugged. 'At least I'm honest enough to admit that there are times when I have trouble forgetting that you're a million-dollar baby who, in normal circumstances, would never give a guy like me the time of day.' His voice deepened. 'You're a very beautiful and desirable woman. Even when you look like a red-eyed, red-nosed, bedraggled puppy.'

Trac fought down the urge to slug him. 'You fascinate me,' she jeered. 'Fortunately, I have no trouble at all forgetting that I detest you.'

He uncoiled his long length from the sofa and stood up, disbelief plain on his face. 'Liar.' Ignoring her indignant gasp, he added, 'Life will be more pleasant if we maintain a middle ground somewhere between the bedroom and the battlefield.'

Embarrassment at her actions had scarcely lessened the next morning as Tracy sat at her workbench. She had spent the remainder of the previous evening avoiding Neil. Not difficult, because he seemed to have no more inclination to seek out her company than she did his. As she'd finished her unpacking she'd been aware of his voice in the background. Long phone calls. To whom? What did she know about Neil other than that he was Jake Archer's emissary, vouched for by Ed Baldwin? Maybe he had a wife and children back in New York. Just because he'd kissed her, it didn't mean he was free to do so.

Any more than the fact that she'd kissed him back meant she liked him. She couldn't decide which was worse—the kiss or the way she'd broken down and cried. As much as she hated to agree with anything Neil said, she had been indulging in self-pity. The immediate past had been sheer living hell, and throughout the whole ordeal she'd held her head up so high that her neck literally ached from the strain. To one more accustomed to reading about herself in the society pages, the horrible black headlines over stories that wildly speculated about every aspect of the tragedy were as painful as they were gross invasions of her privacy.

All she had wanted was to mourn in peace, but reporters had camped on her doorstep to thrust microphones into her face the minute she'd appeared. Finally the unceasing morbid interest in the tragedy, coupled with the loud whispers and pointing fingers that met her every appearance in public, had driven her headlong into flight. She'd escaped thankfully to the sanctuary offered by her stepfather's sister in Ireland.

Only to have the fall-out from the tragedy follow her. Stan Warner's will left all his earthly possessions, in the event if his wife predeceasing him, to his sister. Sally O'Brien had been as embarrassed as she was gratified by her brother's will. She'd wanted to share with Tracy, but Tracy's stubborn pride had prevented her from accepting more from her stepaunt than a place of temporary refuge.

Tracy looked around her workshop with pride. If certain people wanted to believe that being the daughter of the very rich Jake Archer and stepdaughter of the upper-crust Stan Warner magically conferred wealth on her, let them. Pulling her jigsaw into position, she had to admit that she'd never met anyone so determinedly prejudiced against her as Neil was. No doubt due to his law background. Didn't lawyers have to stick with their clients whether they believed them guilty or not? Sides had been drawn up, and Neil was squarely on Jake Archer's side. Loyalty was an admirable quality, but Neil carried it to excess.

Reluctantly Tracy conceded that he'd been kind enough when he'd found her crying in the kitchen, even if his sympathy *had* evaporated quicker than her tears. Adjusting her safety glasses, she switched on the saw. It whined loudly as tiny teeth cut along the lines she'd drawn on the wood. As Neil frequently pointed out, he wasn't in Colorado to sympathise with her. Switching off the saw, she inspected the gingerbread trim. The tragedy had her way behind schedule. Fortunately the woman who'd commissioned this house has been understanding.

Heavy footsteps clattered down the basement steps. 'Here you are.' Neil came through the storage area into her brightly lit work room and stopped abruptly. 'What's all this?'

'What I dabble in,' Tracy said, sarcastically repeating his earlier words in Ed's office. She tugged at the mask that covered her nose and mouth.

Neil moved closer, intent on the house sitting on the table. 'What's this?'

'A doll's house.' His presence seemed to shrink her workshop, while the odour of turpentine and paint and glue that was a permanent fixture in the room failed to blot out his musky scent.

'You make toys?' Reaching out a finger, he pushed open the front door.

'No. I make houses for adults—collectors. All my houses are built to exact scale. One inch equals one foot.'

Neil looked around the well-equipped workroom with its peg-board and shelves for her tools and paints, bins for her supplies and large benches for various tasks. 'You certainly have a lot of professional-looking equipment for a hobby.'

'It's not a hobby. It's how I make my living.'

Neil laughed. 'You couldn't keep yourself in bubble bath doing something like this.'

'That'll all you know,' Tracy said furiously. 'I'm getting ten thousand dollars for this particular house.'

He whistled in surprise. 'Why would anyone pay ten thousand dollars for a house no one but Thumbelina could live in?'

'Nostalgia. One of her great-grandfathers made a fortune mining gold, and he built a palatial "Queen Anne" Victorian mansion in Cripple Creek, Colorado. Unfortunately, a disastrous fire in 1896 burned much of Cripple Creek to the ground, including the mansion. Her grandmother was in her teens then, and in later years she used to entertain my client with fascinating stories about liviing in that house.' Tracy rubbed her finger down one of the many off-centre turrets. 'My client wants to recapture something of her past, and so she asked me to rebuild the mansion in miniature. She loaned me some old, faded letters and tintypes and I've spent hours of research at the library.'

'Incredible,' Neil murmured, walking around to the open back of the house, his feet stirring up the thick covering of sawdust on the floor. 'How long does a house like this take you?' Curiously he opened and shut the small window in the parlour.

'Six to eight months.'

'That hardly adds up to enough to support your life-style. This house, a designer wardrobe. The trip to Ireland.'

'I admit that I've lived in this house rent-free, but I paid all my own bills. As for my clothes, my mother liked to buy me presents. Was there anything wrong with that?'

'And the trip to Europe?' he pressed.

'Cleaned out my savings. Are you satisfied? When I told you in Ed's office that I was broke, it was the truth.'

'That's why you're fighting your father for your mother's estate.'

'I'm merely complying with his orders so that I can keep my home. Surely you don't call that fighting?'

'Why aren't you fighting? I'd have expected you to hire some high-priced lawyer and take Jake to court.'

'My mother's name has been dragged through enough mud. If it weren't for this place, I'd tell Jake Archer to go to hell.'

'That and the money,' Neil said relentlessly.

Tracy shrugged. 'There's no use my disagreeing with you. You've made up your mind to dislike me.' She picked up her stencil and began tracing out more gingerbread trim. 'I can't help but wonder why. . .oh. . .' She rounded her eyes and pressed her fingers against her mouth as if struck by a sudden thought. 'You probably had a rich fiancée back east who dumped you for someone with more money. I'll bet I remind you of her.'

Neil snorted. 'Changing the subject?'

'Not at all. There must be some reason why you're so eager to accuse me of avarice at every opportunity. What do I have to do to convince you that I'm just your average working girl?'

'The average working girl doesn't receive an allowance fit for a princess,' Neil said flatly.

'And what is that supposed to mean?' She tossed her pencil on to the workbench and swivelled on her stool to face Neil.

'I know to the penny how much money Jake sent your mom every month in order to support your débutante life-style.'

'Not a single one,' Tracy denied. 'He never sent her any money. Don't you think I'd know?' She almost physically flinched at the hard expression in his eyes. 'I see. You think I do know.'

'Drop the act, Tracy. I've seen your bills. College, travel, clothes. You and your mother have been spending Jake's money as if it grew on trees. Not content with the handsome divorce settlement she won, your mother billed him for every penny of your very expensive upbringing.'

'I don't believe you.' She hunched her shoulders against the painful barrage of Neil's accusations. 'Mother told me he refused us money, that—that he didn't care about us.'

'Check the court records yourself. Why would I lie about something so easy for you to disprove?' The sharp edge to his voice slashed at Tracy. 'Your mother took Jake for every dime he had when she left him.'

'He left her! Why are you saying these things?'

'Because they're true. She kicked him out of their house, and then your saintly grandfather got him kicked out of Denver.'

Tracy shook her head from side to side. 'You're lying.'

'He was lucky that his law firm had an office in New York and was willing to let him move there. Your grandfather wanted him fired.'

'No.' She stood up gripping the edge of her work-bench to give her support. He couldn't make her listen to all these lies. They *were* lies. She turned away from him, fighting the bitter bile that threatened to choke her. 'I don't know why you're telling me these things when you know they're not true, but. . .'

'When are you going to admit——?'

She cut him off with a defensive gesture. 'No, please. . .' She couldn't stay and listen to any more. Neil started to say something but, shaking her head, Tracy stumbled from the room.

Lying on her bed, her body felt bruised and battered from Neil's revelations. She stared at the ceiling. An old-fashioned floral wallpaper covered it and the walls, blending the hodgepodge of nooks and crannies into a warm, intimate haven. Only it didn't feel like a haven today, as Neil's accusing voice echoed loudly in her ears.

The clock on the bedside-table loudly ticked off the passing minutes. Tick tock. Tick tock. Li-ar. Li-ar. Li-ar. But, who was lying? She couldn't ask her mother; her mother was dead. Closing her eyes, she remembered the night before she'd left for college on the east coast. She'd been packing when her mother had come into her bedroom. It had been immediately evident that her mother had something on her mind, and Tracy had been resigned to listening to a lecture about sex. Instead her mother had told her that her father had refused to send money to a daughter he'd never loved, a daughter he'd forgotten he ever had. She'd told Tracy that he had a new wife and a stepson. Tracy had often wondered why her mother had selected that particular moment to tell her something that her mother must have known for some time, but she couldn't have been lying. Neil was. He wouldn't have said those things if her mother were still alive.

Why did Neil have to lie? Why did he want to hurt her? The answer came slowly. Neil had told her himself. He was physically attracted to her. And he didn't want to be. He feared the attraction, saw it as a weakness, so he was striking back, hurting her to make himself feel stronger. She hadn't liked him, but she hadn't expected him to be weak and petty. Tracy thrust aside any feelings of disappointment. Neil's feet of clay were nothing to her.

A loud knock sounded at her bedroom door. Without turning her head, she mumbled at Neil to go away.

Instead he stuck his head around the door. 'Can I come in?'

'No.'

Ignoring her refusal, he moved to the bed and sat gingerly on the edge of the mattress. 'You didn't know,' he said, his words more a statement than a question.

Tracy shut her eyes. 'There was nothing to know.'

'The minute I opened my big mouth, I could tell

by the look on your face that what I was saying was a complete shock to you. But did that shut me up? No, I had to keep going, rub your nose in it.' There was a long pause. 'I wanted to hurt you.'

CHAPTER FOUR

TRACY's eyes shot open. 'You admit it?'

Neil took her nearest hand into his. 'I met your father, Jake Archer, during my first year in law school.' His grip tightened painfully around Tracy's fingers at her involuntary recoil. 'My dad was dead and my mom was a schoolteacher. There wasn't a lot of money. My younger sister and I worked our way through college. She baby-sat and typed while I did everything from canning fish in Alaska during the summer to waiting tables in the dormitories during the school year. I spent so much time working that as times I could hardly keep awake in class because I'd been up so late trying to get my studying done the night before.' A small muscle twitched along his jawline. 'Jake was a guest lecturer in one of my classes. Shortly after that he hired me for odd jobs, and when I graduated from law school he took me into his firm. If it wasn't for Jake, I'm not sure that I could have made it.'

Her hand ached in Neil's tight grasp. 'What does that have to do with me?'

'I'd go to the stake for Jake, but he's never asked me for anything in exchange. Until now, when he asked me to come out here and watch over you—not as part of my job, but as a personal favour.' He turned her hand over, studying her short, stubby, craftsman nails. 'My sister was always grateful for anything that Mom and I could do to help her out. I couldn't help but compare her with you, a spoiled brat who never bothered to acknowledge her father's existence. I couldn't turn Jake down, so I decided I'd come out here and show the high and mighty Tracy Warner that she couldn't always have life her way.'

Tracy finally managed to free her hand. 'I see.'

'Do you?' Neil's lips turned up fleetingly. More grimace than smile. 'That's more than I do. You walk into the house where your mother was murdered without even flinching. Your stepfather is accused of heinous crimes and you say you question his guilt, but you do nothing about it. A tough old broad, or you just don't give a damn—which is it? I've seen you angry, stubborn, proud. To look at you a man would expect softness and tenderness, but even when we were kissing you were fierce, practically attacking me.'

Anger flicked along her veins. 'And you resented the fact that I didn't melt in your arms.'

'Actually,' he said drily, 'I resented wanting you to. It usually takes more than a pretty face to interest me.'

She fought to keep her voice cool. 'Well, don't worry, little boy, I'll try and tone down my sexual magnetism in your presence so you don't get overheated. There'll be no more need for you to lie.'

Neil frowned and stood up abruptly. 'You're like a beautiful package wrapped in hard, glossy paper. I can't help but wonder what I'd find if I tore away the paper and opened the box. Would there be anybody inside?' He paused at the open doorway, his back to her. 'And just for the record, I've never lied to you.'

One of you lied. The words went round and round in Tracy's head. Neil or her mother. Her mother or Neil. Neil admitted that he'd wanted to hurt her. Her mother loved her. And her mother hated Jake

Archer. The thought came from deep within Tracy's subconscious. Had her mother hated Jake Archer enough that she would have done anything to keep his daughter from him? Reluctantly, Tracy had to admit that the answer was yes. Even something as shameful as lying to her daughter.

Tracy squeezed her eyes tightly shut. How had her mother known? Had Tracy given away her intent by some careless word or deed? Because one of the first things that Tracy had intended to do after she'd settled in at the college was to contact her father and ask him why he'd left her, why he'd never contacted her. But her mother's conversation had dynamited that intention. Her mother had deliberately chosen that particular moment to blacken Jake Archer's name. Salty tears stung the back of her eyelids. Was it possible that her mother was the liar, not Neil?

The divorce had taken place years ago, but there would be records. She could find out. She had to know. From somewhere came the unwelcome memory of a grotesque skull—a grinning mask that hid the emptiness inside. Except that there was no grin on her face, Tracy felt that same emptiness inside her. Neil was right; there was nobody there. She was nobody to those who should have cared about her. Other fathers didn't abandon their daughters. Other stepfathers loved their stepdaughtes. Other mothers. . .she caught back a sob. If her mother hated her former husband so much that hurting him took priority over everything, including the feelings of her own daughter. . .no, that was too painful to think about.

Thinking about Neil was little better. She'd been right. Neil didn't dislike all rich girls; his animosity was reserved for Jake Archer's daughter. He'd been honest enough about that. A heavy depression weighted down her bones. Hatred. A loathsome, evil emotion that twisted people's minds until they were incapable of rational behaviour. Her mother hating Jake Archer. Jake hating them all: her mother, her grandparents, even this house. And Neil hating her. For things that had happened in the past, things she had had no control over, things she knew nothing about. Someone hating her mother and stepfather enough to murder them? The seeds of hatred, so easily sown, so difficult to eradicate.

Forcing herself to her feet she thrust aside her melancholy thoughts. There was no changing the past. Her mother, Jake Archer, even Neil, they'd all made their choices. The important thing was that she must not allow their choices to influence her. The present, her future, those were up to her.

She was standing in front of the window staring blankly outside when a flash of blue from the edge of the clearing behind her house caught her eye. The bluebirds were back. A sign of spring. Ever since she'd moved down here, the bluebirds had returned in April. She kept watching and was soon rewarded by the reappearance of the male, his plumage an electrifying blue in the sunshine as he dived to the ground for an insect. A world that held bluebirds could not be completely without hope.

'Tracy. . .'

The unexpected sound of Neil's voice startled her, and she jumped. 'Do you have to sneak up on me?' she demanded, wiping the streak of red paint from a miniature window pane.

'I wasn't sneaking,' Neil disputed. 'You were so lost in your work. . .' He wrinkled up his nose.

'Phew. How can you stand that paint smell?' A rush of cold air invaded the workroom as he opened a window.

'Did it ever occur to you that I might not want that window open? Maybe I prefer asphyxiation to freezing to death.' She hadn't forgiven him for his accusations of the previous day.

Neil gave her a withering look. 'Don't you mean that if I want it open, you want it closed?'

'It's my workshop and I'll decide the conditions. You needn't think that you can waltz in here and run my life just because I'm forced to let you play at being a bodyguard.'

'I may not have to *play*,' sarcasm underlined the last word, 'for much longer.'

Tracy whirled to face him. 'Why? What's happened? Have the police found out something?'

'Such eagerness to clear your stepfather,' Neil mocked. 'Could it be that you really do care, or is it the possibility of my departure that excites you?'

'The latter!' Tracy snapped.

'In that case,' Neil dismissed her, turning away, 'I thought you might be interested in today's mail, but apparently the solution to our petty little crime holds no interest for you.'

'Wait.' Mail was not delivered to Tracy's home, and Neil had gone to the post office yesterday and today to pick it up, reminding her each time to stay inside the locked house until he returned. Yesterday he'd depositied her letters on the kitchen-table where she'd read them when she came up for lunch. 'What's so special about today's mail?'

Neil turned slowly around. 'Never mind. You said your only interest was in getting rid of me.'

'You know very well I said that to annoy you.'

'You mean you *are* interested in clearing Stan's name?'

Tracy threw her brush on the table, ignoring the splash of red paint. 'I'm getting sick and tired of your accusations and insinuations. Let me tell you something, Neil Charles, and you listen good, because I don't ever want to have to say it again. Whether or not I loved my mother is none of your business. As it happens, I did, and. . .' she cleared her throat of a sudden constriction '. . .I miss her very much. And Stan was good to me.' She faced Neil defiantly. 'You've made up your mind about me, and nothing I say or do is going to change it. If I cry, you accuse me of self-pity; if I don't cry, you say I'm callous. It may surprise you to hear this, but I don't give a damn what you think about me. Your opinions may carry weight with—with the Supreme Court, but they don't mean a thing around here.' She put out her hand. 'Let me see what was so interesting in the mail.'

'What makes you think that there was anything interesting?'

'You said so.'

'But you don't give a damn about my humble opinion.' He flashed a supercilious smile. 'Remember?'

Tracy slid off her stool. 'Let me guess. I've hurt your feelings. You can say whatever you want about me, but if I return the favour, you're going to pout like a little boy.' She snapped her fingers under his nose. 'Give me the mail.'

'Ah, reverting to type, I see. Her ladyship snapping her fingers and expecting the peons to do her bidding.' Hooded eyes held an angry gleam. 'In a pig's eye.' Dangling a small envelope high over his head, he ordered, 'Ask nicely.'

'Please,' she ground out between her teeth.

He shook his head. 'You need practice. Try again.'

'I don't intend to beg.'

'Oh, no?' he taunted softly.

Clenching her fists spasmodically at her sides, Tracy refused to give Neil the satisfaction of goading her into losing her temper. As much as she wanted to smack his smirking face, she knew she'd never get her hands on that envelope if she did. And she very much wanted to see what was inside. Neil was waiting. Suddenly she knew how to get the envelope and teach Neil a lesson at the same time. Wiping her hands on her already dirty jeans, she moved over to him and placed her hands lightly on his chest. His heart beat rhythmically against her palms. 'Neil,' she said, in a low, sultry voice, 'may I have the mail now?' Head bent low, she peered up at him from beneath dark lashes. 'Please.' One hand toyed with his shirt buttons. The finger of her other hand tiptoed their way up his arm towards the hand holding the mysterious envelope.

Neil gave an odd little laugh. 'You play dirty,' he said, pulling her up against his firm body, his hands warm against her hips. He'd guessed, she realised in dismay, before his lips claimed hers, causing her entire insides to dip precipitously. The purpose of her manoeuvre was forgotten as Tracy buried her hands in Neil's silky brown hair, closing her eyes to escape from the dangerous blaze that burned in his. The paint odour faded away to be replaced by the sensual aroma of sandalwood that Tracy had already come to associate with Neil. The chill of the room was forgotten as he persuaded her lips to part, the erotic touch of his tongue sending pulsating flames of fire to the very core of her being. She burned with the heat, her bones melted and useless so that she had to cling to him for support.

Neil slid one hand inside the collar of her old flannel shirt, his fingers scorching her skin. Buttons slipped easily through stretched and worn buttonholes. As the chilled air from the open window flowed over her heated skin, Neil swallowed her murmur of protest and wrapped his large hands possessively around her lace-covered breasts, his thumbs curling about the sensitive tips. She uttered a low cry of pleasure at the intimate touch.

Neil stepped away, releasing her. The imprint of his hands was warm on her breasts. 'You don't do things half-way, do you?' he said hoarsely. 'A simple please would have sufficed. Here.'

She stared blankly, first at him, then at the envelope he had thrust between them.

'The mail,' he said impatiently. 'Wasn't that the point of your little seduction?'

Shattered by the explosive impact of Neil's kiss, Tracy gave him a look of horror. 'I don't even like you,' she said, disbelief mingled with shock in her voice as she clasped the front of her shirt together.

'Disconcerting, isn't it?'

'Disconcerting? It's worse than that! It's. . .it's. . .'

'Horrible, disgusting, appalling,' Neil suggested.

His jeering voice was a dash of iced water on her heated emotions. 'You mock everything,' she said bitterly, starting to turn away.

Neil's hand on her arm detained her. 'You're making too much of it.'

She looked at him incredulously. 'Too much?' she

cried. 'I let a man I don't know, I don't like, kiss me and. . .and. . .'

'Make love to you?'

'Yes.' She shrugged out of his grasp. Head down, she buttoned up her shirt and tucked the tail back into her jeans. 'I suppose now you think I'm a tramp in addition to all my other fine qualities.'

'I thought you didn't give a damn about what I think.'

'I don't!' she flashed, glaring defiantly at him.

'Then why are you so upset about enjoying a couple of kisses?'

'I didn't enjoy. . .' Her disclaimer was met with a raised eyebrow so eloquent of disbelief that she stopped mid-sentence. 'All it means is that you're a lot more experienced than I am,' she charged. 'All I wanted——'

'Was the envelope,' Neil interrupted. 'And you thought that you could distract me long enough to grab it. I couldn't resist teasing you a little.'

Tracy stiffened with resentment. She had totally lost control in Neil's arms, and he'd been merely toying with her. 'I hope you enjoyed your little joke,' she said.

Neil reached over and traced her clenched jaw with a long finger. 'As a matter of fact, I did.'

She jerked her head away from his touch. 'More revenge because I was born wealthy and you weren't? Why stop with a mere kiss? You knew you were in control. Why didn't you finish ripping off my clothes, throw me on the floor and—and take me?'

'Take you where?'

Neil's dry voice squelched her dramatic moment and she glowered at him. 'You know very well what I mean.'

He grinned, a masterpiece of arrogant self-confidence. 'A concrete floor covered with wood shavings and sawdust is not my idea of a cushy love-nest.'

'I didn't realise you were so fastidious.'

'Too fastidious to bed a woman I don't like, no matter how much she tempts me,' he retorted.

'I wasn't tempting you.'

'Besides,' he said, disregarding her denial, 'Jake didn't send me out here to enjoy myself in your bedroom.'

'I see.' Tracy turned to her work-table and picked up the abandoned brush, clenching it in her fist. 'It's OK if you call me names, condemn me with every word out of your mouth, judge me on a past you know nothing about, infuriate me, accuse me of vile behaviour and do your best to h-hurt me. . .' Her voice shaking with rage, she added, 'Jake Archer didn't send you out here to protect me. He sent you out here to torment me, but even he draws the line at your sleeping with me.' Her diatribe was met with silence. Because he couldn't deny it, Tracy told herself furiously as she attacked the woodwork in the tiny dining-room with red paint. Why was he just standing there like a dummy? If he didn't have anything to say, he could just leave. The sound of his breathing irritated her.

Neil broke the prolonged silence. 'Jake would never condone my behaviour. Any of it.' There was a short pause. 'When clients come into my office, I pride myself on my ability to listen to their stories without making judgements. You probably find that hard to believe. . .'

'I do.'

He ignored her curt comment. 'We got off to a bad start. You were angry about the will and your father's conditions, and lashed out at me. I didn't want to be here, and blamed you. We were bonfires waiting to be lit, and each supplied the other's match. That initial flare-up probably wouldn't have amounted to much if it hadn't been for the damnable need to establish my credentials as your boyfriend at the Baldwins' party. Forced to deny our real emotions, it shouldn't have come as any surprise that when we kissed it was instant combustion.' His raised hand cut off Tracy's objection. 'It was and you know it.'

'I suppose you're trying to make a point here.'

'As a matter of fact, I am. I suggest that we start all over. You might be in danger and I'm supposed to protect you. Your background, my background, they don't matter.'

'I can't just forget——'

'Yes, you can,' Neil said. 'Until this matter is settled. Call it a temporary truce. OK?'

Tracy looked down at his extended hand and then up into his face. 'Why?'

'For your own safety.'

Tracy caught her breath and edged away until the hard rim of the workbench jabbed her in the back. 'A-are you th-threatening me?' she stammered.

'Threatening you? With what?'

The genuine bafflement in his eyes convinced Tracy she'd made an error. 'Never mind,' she said hastily.

Neil's mouth twisted in a grim smile as he dropped his hand. 'I can guess. Let me assure you, Miss Warner, that you are safe from me, truce or no truce. I don't sleep with cold, heartless women who live by arbitrary social rules instead of the golden rule, and who have iced-water in their veins.'

Tracy concentrated on her painting, trying to

ignore the pain of Neil's angry words. He had offered a suspension of their hostilities, but she'd dynamited his offer with her suspicions. It could be weeks before the police found the real murderer. Meanwhile, if the days loomed drearily before her, she had no one to blame but herself. Absorbed in self-condemnation, she didn't realise at first that Neil was talking to her. 'What?'

'I said, this is a colourful house.' His impersonal tone of voice told her the previous subject was closed.

'The Victorians loved colour.' She hadn't meant to sound so cold and abrupt. With some thought of making amends, she added, 'Colour technology made giant strides during that time, and colour reproductions in books introduced people to new dyes.' Finishing the trim, Tracy tapped the lid back on the paint-can.

'You must do a lot of research.' He walked around the workbench and peeked through the front door of the small house.

'I try to be as accurate as possible.'

'It's a shame that the original house burned down. I wonder why they never tried to rebuild it?'

'Apparently the owner had had a tremendous argument with his father and brothers, and left Texas under somewhat shaky circumstances. He didn't want to go back, but his wife was also from the south and she hated the cold winters in Cripple Creek. She convinced him that the house burning was an omen, so he sold the mine and they moved back to Texas, where they bought some land and started a very successful cattle ranch, and his family forgave him all.' Tracy swished her brush in a jar of thinner. 'Aren't you going to say something clever about money buying forgiveness?'

'I was thinking more along the lines that it was nice they buried the hatchet and gave each other a second chance.'

Tracy glanced across the workbench at Neil, and then quickly looked away. His deliberate gaze left no doubt that he was aiming his comment directly at her. 'Probably because they weren't cold and heartless women who ignored the golden rule and had iced water in their veins,' she said.

'Do you want me to apologise?'

'You'd probably choke on it.'

'Just as you'd choke on apologising for thinking I'm the type of person who'd assault a woman just because she made me mad?'

Tracy felt the colour drain from her face. 'I didn't mean that, exactly.'

'What did you mean, exactly?'

She swallowed hard. 'I guess I did mean that,' she said in a small voice. 'It sounds so much worse when you put it into words. I had no right, no reason. . .You might not believe me, but I truly am sorry.'

'If you had said it out of anger to provoke me, that would be one thing. But you really believed it. Never mind,' he said as she opened her mouth. 'If I've behaved so badly that you're afraid of me, it's not your fault. It's mine.' He sighed heavily. 'I never intended to terrify you.'

The note of mortification in his voice disturbed Tracy. Harsh and critical of her Neil had undoubtedly been, but he had never given her a reason to fear him. In normal circumstances she would never have jumped to such an insulting and erroneous conclusion. But then, nothing about her life these past few months could be called normal. But how did one explain that to Neil? 'I wasn't exactly terrified,' she finally said.

'Damn it, Tracy.' He jammed his hands in his pockets and glared across the workbench at her. 'I donate money to the zoo, help little old ladies across the street and buy Girl Scout cookies. How could you be afraid of me?' he shouted. 'I'm totally harmless.'

The ferocious look on his face contrasted so absurdly with his claim that Tracy was unable to quell the bubble of laughter that popped out. 'In fact, you're nothing but a pussycat.'

A reluctant smile appeared at the corners of his mouth. 'You do seem to bring out the worst in me.' He leaned around the small house and extended his hand towards Tracy. 'And you have seen my worst. I promise. You have nothing to fear from me.' His hand was steady, but a small muscle twitching in his wrist betrayed his tension.

Slowly Tracy placed her hand in his. 'I believe you.'

His hand closed painfully over hers. 'Thank you.' He turned her hand over. One finger traced her lifeline. 'I should have explained what I meant by your safety.'

'That isn't necessary.' She screwed the cap back on the paint thinner, an excuse to escape Neil's grip. Her palm tingled where he'd touched it.

'Yes, it is. Our feuding was distracting my attention from my assignment. Jake sent me out here to ensure that his daughter was safe. By allowing myself to be side-tracked, I was letting him down.'

Tracy concentrated on wiping dry her brush. 'Something I've wondered about. . .'

'What?'

'Why the belated interest in my safety? It's been

over three months since the. . .since it happened, and no one has been worried about me before.'

'Did you ever go anywhere alone in Ireland?'

'No, but that was because Aunt Sally was afraid that I might get lost. . .oh,' she said, a flat note in her voice.

'Jake called her,' Neil confirmed. 'He was on vacation himself when the tragedy occurred. He knew about it, of course, but had no reason to doubt the newspaper account until he returned to his office. There was a letter there from Stan Warner. He'd decided to sell the business. . .'

'Sell? I never knew that.'

'He was being very hush-hush about the whole thing. That's why he'd contacted Jake. He hinted at something wrong and wanted Jake's advice. Someone from out of town who didn't know the players, he said. Apparently the company holds the patent on some dinky little part that they sell to the government. That contract alone makes the company very attractive to potential buyers. If Warner needed money, all he had to do was sell the company. Even after paying off the stockholders, he stood to make a mint. That letter started Jake thinking, and then that same day someone tried to break into your parents' home.'

'The police told me, but I thought it was just a burglar. Someone who'd read the papers and thought it was empty.'

'Maybe. Or maybe someone who thought that Warner had left behind some incriminating evidence. Just the suspicion was enough to send Jake into action. A call to your Aunt Sally, the Baldwins. . .'

'Then it wasn't a coincidence that Ed was in New York when I landed and just happened to have space for me on the corporate plane back to Denver.' Another thought occurred to her. 'What if I'd refused to comply with Jake's orders? Said to heck with the house and moved into an apartment.'

Neil refused to meet her eyes. 'Actually, I don't think that possibility occurred to anyone. Over the years Stan Warner put a number of properties in your mother's name. Her estate is—er—substantial.'

'I see,' said Tracy, wondering why his disclosure should be such a painful surprise. Neil had never hidden his belief that she was only after the money.

'In any case,' Neil broke the uncomfortable silence, 'today's mail seems to support Jake's theory that Warner is innocent.' He picked up the envelope.

Tracy snatched it from his hand. The flap had already been ripped open and she removed a small card from inside. Black-lettered words leapt up at her.

> WANT TO KNOW THE TRUTH ABOUT STAN WARNER? MEET ME AT THE ESTEMERE GAZEBO 8:30 THURS. NIGHT. COME ALONE.

Neil was studying the envelope. 'Addressed to me care of you, and postmarked in Denver yesterday.'

'This is crazy,' Tracy protested. 'Who knows you're here?'

'Everyone at the Baldwins' party,' Neil said, walking from her workroom.

'I can't believe that any of those people are the type to be skulking around in the dark whispering secrets to you.' Tracy followed him up the stairs.

'I suppose it's easier to believe that your stepfather is a thief and a murderer.'

'No, of course not, but I know these people, they're. . .'

'Rich, cultured, sophisticated? Above committing a social *faux pas* like theft and murder?' Neil asked with biting sarcasm. Before Tracy could protest, he whirled towards her. 'Damn it, Tracy, it has to be someone who knows I'm down here.'

'That could be lots of people. Someone who heard from someone who was at the party. News travels fast by word of mouth. Blake might have mentioned it to someone at the plant.'

'Why me?' Neil demanded, pacing the length of the kitchen.

'Why would Blake talk about you?' Tracy asked.

'No, why send the note to me? Why not the police? Or Campbell, or someone else at the plant? Why not you? Why would anyone want to talk to me about the crime? A stranger?'

'Maybe,' Tracy said slowly, 'that's why. Whoever sent that note doesn't want his identity known. Blake, the police, me—we would recognise him. You're a stranger. He feels safer.'

Neil gave her a look of surprise. 'Sherlock Holmes, as I live and breathe! I think you're right.'

'You needn't act so dumbfounded,' Tracy said tartly.

Neil grinned, but refused to debate the point. 'Tell me how to get to the town of Estemere, and where's the gazebo?'

'Estemere isn't a town. It's the name of an old mansion.'

'In Denver?'

'No, here in Palmer Lake.'

'Tell me about it.'

'You've seen it. That old house with a million turrets and gables. A wealthy dentist named Thompson built it back in the 1880s with everything from a billiard-room to an observatory.'

'Yeah, I think I remember it. Where's the gazebo?'

'It's part of the stone and iron fence along the front.'

'I wonder why our mysterious letter-writer chose it?'

'Perhaps it seemed fitting. Dr Thompson slunk out of town under mysterious financial circumstances.' An earlier comment of Neil's came back to her. 'Do you think the murderer wrote this?'

'No, where would be the sense in that? The murderer's best bet is simply to lie low, not to do something stupid that might cause the police to suspect that Stan wasn't the culprit. What made you think that?'

'When I said that no one at the party was the type to skulk around in the dark, you immediately suggested that being in high society didn't exclude them from being murderers and thieves.'

'Think about it,' Neil advised, leaning against a cabinet and giving her a steady look. 'If Stan didn't steal the money from his plant, who was in a position to do so? Six men.' He named them. 'All of them in your social circle.'

'That's absurd,' Tracy protested. 'Some of those men have been with Stan since he took over the business. Blake has been here the shortest time, and he and Stan had become very close. You're not going to tell me that Blake murdered my mother?'

'I'm not going to tell you anything. I'm hoping that our friend here,' he waved the envelope, 'is going to tell me.'

'Have you called the police yet about the note?'

'No, and I'm not going to. If you're right about our mysterious correspondent wanting to hide his identity, the last thing I want is a police stake-out scaring him away. If they do, I might never find out what this guy knows.'

'Then I'm going with you.'

'The hell you are.'

Tracy started to argue, but one look at Neil's determined face told her that she would lose the argument. She'd have to think of some other way around him. 'All right. I'm too hungry to argue with you anyway. What's for lunch?'

'It won't work,' Neil said, walking to the refrigerator. 'Whatever you're planning in that devious mind of yours, forget it. I said I'm going alone and that's final.'

'So who's arguing with you?' Tracy took a bite out of the enormous salad that Neil had set in front of her.

'I'm beginning to recognise that look on your face.'

'What look?' she asked innocently. Before Neil could tell her, she quickly changed the subject. 'If I have to have a bodyguard, give me one that can cook every time. This is delicious.'

'Cooking is only one of my many talents,' Neil said. 'Another is reading the minds of little girls who are too clever for their own good.'

'OK, smarty pants.' Tracy closed her eyes. 'What am I thinking now?'

'That you want a piece of chocolate cream pie for lunch.'

'I am not.' She opened her eyes in astonishment. 'Why would I be thinking that?'

'Because I bought some at the grocery store and you don't want to hurt my feelings.'

'You bought a pie? World-famous chef that you claim to be, and you bought a pie?'

'Even world-famous chefs need the proper tools,'

he said drily as he collected her dirty plate. 'From the state of your cupboard, I'd say you live on frozen dinners. Can't you cook anything?' he asked, handing her a piece of pie.

'Sure I can. I specialise in beef Wellington, mushrooms stuffed with crab, piped potatoes, broccoli with hollandaise sauce, Caesar salad and strawberries Romanoff.'

'You're kidding.' He dropped back into his chair.

Tracy smiled. 'Actually, I'm not. When I was sixteen I was madly in love with the president of the French club from this boys' academy near where I went to school. I decided the way to really impress him was to invite him over for a dinner that I'd cooked. Poor Mom and Stan. I practised that meal every night for a week. Show me a Caesar salad today and I'll turn green.'

'Was he impressed?'

'Hardly. He couldn't wait to get out of there and go get some real food—a hamburger. He never asked me out again.'

'Was your heart broken?'

Tracy sighed deeply. 'The first of many times.'

'That surprises me.'

'Did you think rich little girls like me don't have hearts?'

Leaning back in his chair, his eyes darkened as he studied her face. 'I thought beautiful girls like you broke hearts.'

'Experience speaking?'

'No. No beautiful girl broke my heart, no rich fiancée dumped me, no wife, no steady girlfriend. Anything else you want to know?'

The gleam of amusement in his eyes told Tracy that he was reading more into her question than she had intended. She would quickly disabuse him of the idea that she had any personal interest in him. Leaning one elbow on the table, she propped her chin in her hand. 'Yes. I've never understood why my—that is, why anyone would think that I'm in any danger.'

'Why kill your mother? Unless the killer believed that she knew something. That Warner told her something. And if she knew, why not you?'

'But I don't know anything,' Tracy insisted.

'I agree that it's unlikely the murderer would seek you out, but Jake doesn't like to take chances.'

'You talk as if he were some kind of saint,' Tracy said petulantly.

Neil burst into laughter. 'Saint Jake? Hardly. He's quick-tempered, stubborn. . .actually, he's a lot like you.'

'Then I'm surprised that you like him,' Tracy retorted.

'He's also loyal, trustworthy, fair and generous to those he loves,' Neil said evenly.

Tracy swallowed over the sudden lump of pain in her throat. 'I wouldn't know about that.'

'You could. Yes,' he insisted as she shook her head, 'swallow that damned pride and fly out to New York. You're alone and he's——'

'Married,' Tracy flashed. 'And he has a stepson.'

Neil gave her a startled look. 'Stepson?'

'I just can picture him. An athletic superstar—probably football. My. . .Jake was a big football star in college. That's how my mother met him. Her parents didn't approve. The poor boy on an athletic scholarship and the sorority butterfly. And their sole issue—a skinny girl who dabbled in lots of sports and didn't excel at any. He'd always wanted a son like himself.'

'If that's true, Jake blew it again. His wife's son had no time for sports in college.'

'Don't tell me,' Tracy grimaced, 'he's brilliant. A Rhodes scholar, or something like that.'

'Actually, he's just your average guy. Nothing special about him at all. In fact, this guy you keep calling Jake's stepson really isn't. . .'

'You don't like him,' Tracy said slowly.

'I didn't say that.'

'You don't have to. I can tell by your tone of voice. Why not?'

'Tracy, I——'

'Never mind. Be loyal to your boss. Tell me about his wife. Or don't you like her either?'

'I like her. So would you.'

'I doubt it. Is she beautiful?'

'Attractive,' he amended. 'Not as beautiful as your mother.'

The words blurted out before Tracy could stop them. 'Is he happy?'

Neil was silent for so long that she thought he hadn't heard the question. Then he sighed. 'Only Jake can answer that question for you.'

'I'm hardly likely to ask him.'

Neil started to reply, then visibly swallowed his words. Shoving back his chair, he stood up abruptly and walked away.

CHAPTER FIVE

TRACY stared at Neil's departing back in disbelief as he stalked unceremoniously from the kitchen. His actions were a rebuff that held all the sting of a slap across the face. The proposed truce had lasted less than two hours.

And it was all Jake Archer's fault. There might be some truth in Neil's claim that Jake had sent her money, but the fact that he'd provided for her, no matter how generously, did not excuse his refusal to maintain any kind of physical ties between them. Duty prompted monthly cheques. Making an effort to write to her, visit her, phone her—that called for love. A love that Jake Archer obviously did not have for his only daughter. He had not made one effort to contact her from the day he'd left his wife. Tracy finally admitted to herself that one small part of her had been expecting, perhaps even hoping, to hear from him when her mother had died. But nothing. A caring, concerned father would have been on the first plane to Denver. Tracy wasn't a cherished daughter; she was a responsibility to be delegated to a junior member of the firm.

Was Neil so blind that he couldn't see that her father didn't want her? Quick tears sprang to her eyes and she furiously dashed them away. What did she care if Neil Charles was a prejudiced, narrow-minded, censorious prig? She didn't care about his stupid old truce anyway. Other people's approval or love—those were crutches to be used by the weak, and no one knew better than she how quickly those crutches could be yanked away. She'd pulled herself off the ground too many times to subject herself to that pain again.

Dumping her dirty dishes in the sink, she stared out of the kitchen window. The male bluebird was darting in and out of the state capital birdhouse. Tracy studied the trees lining the backyard, and was soon rewarded by the sight of a drab blue bird carefully ignoring the male. The female bluebird.

Two hands dropped to her shoulders. Neil had returned. 'What's so interesting out there?' His voice was friendly.

'Bluebirds.' Her voice was cool.

'The dull-coloured one the missus?'

'Yes.' How dared he pretend nothing had happened?

'What's the male all excited about?'

'He's trying to persuade the female to accept him and the nesting site he's found.'

'It looks as if she's playing hard to get.'

'Survival of the fittest. She wants a good provider, a mate she can depend on. This little ritual could go on for days before she'll consent to inspect the house.' Neil was standing so close that she could feel the heat from his body.

'Tracy Warner, student of nature,' he mocked softly. 'You're full of surprises, aren't you?'

Anger could no longer be suppressed. 'I suppose you object to that, too!' She flung his hands from her shoulders.

'It was a compliment. I've never met a woman so quick to take offence.'

She whirled to face him, hands clenched into fists at her waist. 'Quick to take offence?' she gasped.

'When you are rude and insulting. . .all you do is criticise. And then walk out of the room if I dare to disagree with you. I'm sick of it, and sick of you!'

Neil's brows knitted together in a deep frown. 'You think that I was criticising you for refusing to see Jake?'

'Yes.'

'I do think it's tragic,' he said. 'You and Jake have so much to offer each other.' A finger pressed against her lips kept her quiet. 'If I was abrupt in leaving the room, it's because I suddenly remembered I had this.' He held out a recent issue of a popular business magazine. 'There's an article about Jake. I thought that it might answer some of your questions.'

Tracy held the magazine against her chest. 'I—I don't know what to s-say,' she stammered.

There was a teasing light in Neil's eye. 'How about I'm sorry? How about, I won't jump to any more conclusions? How about, I will never yell at you again?'

'I am sorry, but. . .' She eyed him doubtfully. 'Never is a very long time.'

Neil laughed and picked up the envelope. 'Hopefully this will solve all our problems.'

Tracy filled a cake decorator with the last of the special plaster compound that she was using to make the ceiling medallions. A few more flourishes and she was done. Dried, fastened to the ceiling above the light fixtures in the dining-room and parlour, and painted, they would look exactly like their full-size plaster forebears. Lying down her tools, she stretched, trying to work the kinks out of tired muscles.

The intricate job had kept the worrisome questions

at bay, but now they crowded back. Who was planning to meet Neil tonight at Estemere, and why? She and Neil had discussed the note at great length over the past two days, but were no closer to any answers than they had been the day the note had arrived.

Suddenly it occurred to her that anonymous information could easily be delivered through the mail or over the phone. Was there a more sinister reason why the mysterious correspondent wanted to meet Neil face to face? Neil had to inform the police.

Truce or no truce, she should have known he'd never listen to her. The argument raged all day, and it continued unabated at the dinner-table.

'You have no idea what you're getting into. The police——'

'All the police could do is scare away the informant. You saw the note. I was told to come alone.'

'If you won't call the police, then I'm going with you.'

'No, you're not,' Neil said firmly as he piled stroganoff on a plate.

'They were my parents.'

'As you have reminded me excessively ever since I showed you the note. I can't imagine what demon prompted me to do so.'

'I would suggest your better self, but I have yet to see any evidence that you have one,' Tracy retorted. 'This stroganoff is delicious,' she added grudgingly.

'Flattery won't get you anywhere. You're not going.'

'It wasn't flattery.' She took another bite. 'I meant it.'

'Careful,' Neil chided. 'Dinner will stick in your throat.'

Tracy took a roll from the basket Neil held out.

'How rude not to say thank you when you're complimented.'

A fleeting smile crossed Neil's face. 'Guilty as charged, your honour. The defence pleads diminished responsibility.'

'Defence?' Tracy questioned. 'And here all along I thought you were the prosecution. What is diminished responsibility?'

'It means that I'm not totally responsible for my actions. One minute you're berating me, the next minute complimenting me. Is it any wonder that I'm occasionally at a loss for words?'

'I doubt if you've been at a loss for words since you started to talk,' Tracy said drily. 'Is that why you became a lawyer? So you could always have the last word?'

'Aren't you forgetting Grandmother's dictum about disguising your true feelings?'

'She meant with people who counted,' Tracy said smoothly.

Neil grinned and ducked. 'A direct hit.'

His words reminded her of his evening appointment. 'I don't think you ought to go. It's too dangerous.'

'There's no danger. As far as everyone knows, I'm nothing more than your fiancé.'

'Why not send the information through the mail? Why meet in the dark? Why meet in such a lonely spot? Someone could take a pot shot at you and you'd never know what hit you.'

Neil studied her thoughtfully. 'You really are worried about me.'

'Of course I am. Just because we don't always see eye to eye on things doesn't mean I want you to get hurt, or,' she swallowed, 'killed.'

'I'm not going to get killed or hurt.'

And that, as far as Neil was concerned, was that. Nothing she said could sway him. He was the most stubborn. . .Tracy pitied the poor woman who would ever be dumb enough to marry him.

'You are the most single-minded woman I've met,' Neil complained as she followed him into the front hall after dinner.

Tracy jerked her head towards the window where the fierce wind could be seen whipping the pine trees about in a spring snowstorm. 'No one is going to show up in this kind of weather.'

'Then I won't be in any danger, will I?'

'You're hopeless,' Tracy stormed. 'Stupid, macho. . .go ahead and get shot at.'

He laughed softly. 'Hard-hearted Hannah. You're probably hoping that I'm off to meet my doom just so that you can be rid of me.' He shrugged into his heavy parka.

'That's not true.'

'You mean you don't want to get rid of me?' Neil asked with an inquisitive lift of a dark eyebrow.

'Not that way,' Tracy snapped.

Neil grinned. 'Too bad you're hampered by our truce. If you weren't you could try the same gentle persuasion that was so effective yesterday in your workshop.' He yanked his coat zipper decisively into place. 'If it's any consolation to you,' he said, a wicked gleam in his eyes, 'I'd rather stay here and share your warm, toasty bed, but duty calls. Now, keep the doors locked like a good girl, and I'll be back before you miss me.'

'I wouldn't miss you if you never came back!' Tracy shouted. The shutting of the front door was her only answer.

The stupid, stubborn, pig-headed. . .Tracy muttered to herself as she threw on her winter coat. He needn't think he could order her around—'"Keep the doors locked like a good girl,"' she mimicked under her breath. Waiting until Neil's firm footsteps had descended the front porch steps, she slipped out of the back door. The stinging snowflakes momentarily disorientated her. Edging closer to the house to escape the worst blasts of the wind, she crept to the front yard. Neil was turning the corner at the end of the street. Sticking to the shadows, Tracy moved as swiftly as she could after him. The howling of the wind would cover her footsteps. And anyone else's. The bleak thought quickened her pace. Not that Neil meant anything to her. She would worry about anyone in his situation.

Neil turned the corner and approached Estemere. It would serve him right if he did get shot. He just couldn't resist reminding her that she'd lost her self-control in his arms yesterday. Neil Charles was an egotistical. . .As if she'd called his name, he whirled around. Tracy quickly faded into some bushes along the road. Neil studied his surroundings, pausing to look directly at her. Tracy's coat was dark and there were no street-lights, but her face. . .she dared not breathe. He resumed his walk and she let the air out of her lungs in a giant whoosh. Neil hadn't seen her. He was in front of Estemere now, walking more slowly, his head swivelling from side to side. The ornate iron fence straddling the tall stone wall dwarfed him. Chilling tendrils of fear crawled up Tracy's spine. There were too many places for an ambusher to hide. She'd been foolish to think that following Neil would protect him.

Ahead of her Neil stopped again, and instinctively

she shrank back into the shrubbery across the street. He was in front of the gazebo. Tracy's breath caught. A perfect hiding place if a man wanted to. . .She closed her mind against the unspeakable fear. Neil glanced at his watch and then began pacing back and forth in front of the gazebo. Tracy hunched her shoulders and pulled the hood tighter around her head against the insidious cold. The neighbourhood was dark and the bushes around her rustled ominously. She scanned the vicinity apprehensively, swallowing an impulse to shout at Neil to give it up and return home. Far to the south a dog howled, the mournful sound sending chills up her spine. Nearer at hand two dogs barked. Large dogs. She prayed that they weren't running loose.

Neil continued to pace back and forth in front of the gazebo, pausing occasionally to check his watch. Suddenly he stopped, whirled about and raced down the street towards where Tracy crouched in the bushes. Knowing that he would be furious if he caught her, she hastily tried to scramble further back into the shadows, praying that he wouldn't look over and see her. Haste was her undoing. Her foot caught by a low-lying branch, she was thrust off balance and sent sprawling to the ground, the cracking of branches sounding like shots in the night.

Neil came to an abrupt halt. 'Who is it? Who's there?'

'Me,' Tracy admitted in a faint voice.

Plunging into the bushes, heedless of branches whipping him across his face, Neil yanked her up. Her feet were still entangled and she fell heavily into arms which tightened around her, squeezing the air from her lungs.

'I can't breathe.' Her face was buried in his chest.

Neil loosened his grip, but refused to let her go. He must be furious. Thrusting his hand inside the thick hood that swathed her head, and grabbing her chin, he turned her face up to his and pressed kisses all over her icy cheeks. 'I've never been so glad to see anyone in my whole life,' he muttered. A hard, demanding mouth cut off any reply Tracy might have made.

Tracy was too stunned to resist. The wind beat at them while the snow dampened their faces. When Neil finally dragged his lips away, Tracy gasped, 'I thought you'd be mad.'

'I could wring your blasted neck,' Neil said thickly, his mouth again descending in a savage kiss.

Tracy twisted her head away. 'You have a funny way of showing it.'

A gust of wind pummelled her body and Neil turned them so that his back was to the wind, sheltering her from the worst of the icy blasts. Both his hands were entwined in her hair, and he forced her face up for his inspection. 'What the hell are you doing here? I told you to stay at home.'

'I thought you might need help.'

Neil gave a choke of laughter, and then his hands tightened painfully in her hair, pulling her closer to him in a fierce embrace. There was nothing gentle about the way he closed his mouth on hers, conquering her soft mouth with his thrusting tongue. His kiss, as harsh and primitive as the elements swirling around them, banished Tracy's bewilderment. Neil's lovemaking was his way of punishing her for daring to disobey him. Her eyes teared in the icy wind while frozen snowflakes lashed at her cheeks. Forming her fists into tight balls, she beat on his shoulders, but it was the bright headlight beams of a passing car outlining them against the dark night that finally penetrated Neil's consciousness. He grabbed her hands and held them tight against his chest. 'And how did Palmer Lake's answer to Miss Marple plan to help?' An arm around Tracy's shoulder turned her in the direction of home.

The laughter in his voice disconcerted her. 'I was watching. . .hoping I'd see anyone. . .before. . .' She shivered. 'I didn't realise how dark and creepy it would be.'

Neil squeezed her shoulder. 'Don't worry. No one's here.' His voice was barely audible over the wind.

'How do you know?'

'I saw the flaw behind this note from the first and didn't realise it. Why send it to me? Why not you? Because,' he answered his own question, 'the sender had no intention of telling me anything. He only wanted to get me out of the house.'

'But what would be the point of. . .? Oh. Leaving me alone,' Tracy said flatly.

'Leaving you alone.' His voice was cold and bleak.

'But it didn't work,' Tracy said hastily.

'Only because you elected yourself to be my guardian angel.'

'That's why you're angry,' Tracy guessed. 'Not because I didn't do what you said, but because you think you goofed up.'

'Angry? Where did you get that crazy idea?'

'You said you wanted to wring my neck, and the way you kissed me like that. . .' Her voice trailed off in uncertainty.

'I kissed you because I was so damned relieved to see that you were all right.' The harsh note in his voice betrayed his anxiety. 'Do you have any idea what kind of thoughts were going through my mind when I finally realised why nobody showed up?' His arm tightened painfuly around her shoulders. 'If anything had happened to you, Jake would have had my head.'

'Then it's lucky that I ignored your orders, isn't it?' Tracy said tartly, attempting to shrug free of Neil's arm. 'It would be a shame to annoy the great Jake Archer.'

Neil refused to let her go. 'I didn't mean that the way it sounded, and you know it.' He tipped her chin up with his free arm. 'Fighting with you is getting to be a habit. I'm not sure I could stand the withdrawal pains.'

She might have thought of an answer to that enigmatic remark if she hadn't been so astonished. Besides, she needed to save her energy for walking. Even Neil was silent as they struggled uphill against the wind.

It wasn't until they'd reached her house that he spoke again, and then Tracy was confused by the fluid string of swear words until she looked at her driveway. Fresh tyre prints in the snow were evidence that someone had come and gone in their absence.

'You don't know that it was—was someone who had mischief in mind,' Tracy argued as Neil slipped her wet coat from her shoulders and hung it on the coat-rack.

'It's too late in the year for the Easter Bunny,' Neil retorted, following her into the front parlour and plopping into a comfortable chair. 'I wish I knew the answer to two questions—what it is someone thinks you know, and why the hell it's taking Jake so long to get this mess cleared up.'

As Tracy lay in bed that evening she wished she knew the answer to those questions herself. Sleep was proving elusive. Too many thoughts and emotions ricocheting around inside her head kept her tossing restlessly in bed. Fear and disbelief that she could actually be in danger. Frustration over her inability to pinpoint why she was a threat to anyone. Anger that someone had taken her mother from her. Doubts about her mother and Jake Archer. Questions about things she'd always believed were true.

And finally, reluctantly, she admitted to herself that she felt threatened and confused. Not by some anonymous criminal. By Neil Charles. From the first moment of their meeting he'd bullied his way into her life, making it quite clear that she could like him or hate him but she could never ignore him. He'd called her a coward and then praised her courage. He'd accused her of lying and then demonstrated his own honesty by admitting he was wrong. He had held her in his arms when she'd cried and then called her a cry-baby. He'd laughed at danger to himself, but was terrified when the danger was to her. He'd kissed her and said that the kisses meant nothing.

She traced the outline of her mouth with fingers that trembled. It was only her imagination that her lips were throbbing and swollen. She wouldn't think about Neil's kisses this evening. They were nothing more than a natural expression of relief. People in the grip of strong emotion often acted impulsively. Neil's behaviour once they'd returned to the house had given her no reason to believe otherwise. He had been strictly impersonal, grilling her endlessly on every tiny detail that she could recall about Stan's business and the tragedy. Which was just as well. Neil Charles was here on a job. And when that job was completed he would go back to his own life. A life that included Jake Archer, but not Jake Archer's daughter, she scolded herself before eventually falling into a fitful sleep.

The first moment of wakefulness brought with it an overwhelming sense of fear and helplessness. It wasn't until seconds later that Tracy realised that it was a nightmare which had left her heart pounding and her nightgown cold and clammy against her skin. Pressed against the pillows in the centre of the bed, she noticed her breathing was swift and shallow. The room was dark, but as her eyes adjusted to the night she could pick out the familiar shapes of walls and furniture. Outside, the wind was still blowing in fitful gusts.

Tracy tried to shut out the lingering remnants of the nightmare, but it was too vivid. A dark, shadowy silhouette of a man had pointed a long stick—a gun—at Neil and she'd called to warn him, but the wind had caught her words. She'd run and run, but could get no closer to Neil, whose laughing face had mocked her efforts to catch him. Then, a sharp, cracking sound and she was lying on the ground, on her chest a shocking scarlet blossom with petals that turned pink against the new-fallen snow. Tracy had cried out in anguish and then thankfully awakened.

The nightmare was easy to interpret after the events of the evening. Even though she'd been concerned about Neil meeting with an unknown correspondent, she'd managed to dismiss the idea that she might be in any type of danger. Now she shivered uneasily at the memory of the tyre treads in the driveway. Forcibly she ejected the image from her mind and closed her eyes.

A sharp, cracking sound sent her bolting upright

in bed, her heart pounding sickeningly in her breast. Clutching the covers beneath her chin, she scarcely dared breathe. The sound was repeated, more subdued this time. Tracy slid cautiously from beneath the blankets. The room was cold, but no colder than the icy chill which raced down her spine at the repitition of the ominous-sounding crack. She blessed the fact that her eyes were used to the dark as she edged open her bedroom door. The noise came again from the direction of the front parlour. Someone was in the house. Tantalisingly out of reach in the lower hall was the only telephone. Tracy looked around the upper hallway for a weapon. Her gaze landed upon Neil's closed bedroom door and she breathed a sigh of relief. Neil was downstairs. On the heels of that thought came the realisation that Neil would not be down there stumbling around in the dark.

Tracy had no recollection of moving across the hall, but suddenly she was standing beside Neil's bed. The sound of his steady breathing was loud in the lulls between gusts of wind. He lay on his stomach, rumpled blankets pushed down to his waist. Tracy tentatively tapped one bare shoulder. His skin was warm and smooth. She tapped again. Neil muttered something unintelligible and rolled away from her, the bedsprings protesting loudly beneath him. Tracy froze. From downstairs came an ominous crack, lending urgency to her movements. She crawled over to Neil and stretched out the length of his body, wincing each time a spring creaked. It wouldn't be easy to awaken Neil without alerting the intruder. Pressing against him as tightly as possible, she cupped her hand over his mouth and brought her lips up to his ear. 'Neil.'

Two things happened simultaneously. A warm hand descended to her hip and sharp teeth nipped at the skin of her hand. Before she could jerk her hand away she found herself flat on her back, Neil's face looming over her. 'What an unexpected pleasure,' he murmured. Stunned by his lightning reaction, Tracy was slow to deny his outrageous conclusion. And then it was too late. Fingers woven through her hair held her head immobile as he worked his magic on her lips. Small, nibbling kisses sent her heart racing, the blood pulsing in her ears. His masculine scent filled her nostrils as his warm body pressed her deep into the mattress, his elbows tight against her sides. He kneaded her scalp with a delicate, sensuous touch while his thumbs lightly traced the outer whorls of her ears. Outside, a fierce gust of wind rattled the window panes. Inside, she clung to Neil as he parted her lips, his tongue sending a storm of tumultuous sensations raging throughout her body. He abandoned her mouth, greeting her moan of displeasure with a low chuckle. The sound was deafening in the hushed room and Tracy froze. 'What's the matter?' Neil muttered, his lips pressed against the pulse that beat frantically at the base of her throat.

With Neil's words the reason for her presence in his bed, the reason for the overwhelming need for silence, came back to Tracy in a rush. The intruder. How could she have forgotten? Immediately came the terrifying suspicion that the intruder might already be in the room. Her eyes shot open and she peered fearfully over Neil's shoulder. His bedroom door remained shut; there was no one else in the room. She released her pent-up breath in a rush, her muscles sagging into the mattress.

Neil stiffened. 'Mind tell——' He glared at Tracy above the hand she'd clapped over his mouth.

'Someone in the house,' she mouthed to him.

'Where?' His lips barely moved.

She pointed and the next instant she was alone in the bed, and Neil was across the room, gliding silently past the bedroom door. A sharp crack sounded from downstairs. Tracy leaped soundlessly from the bed. She had no intention of being left behind. If she was going to be murdered in bed, it wasn't going to be in Neil's bed.

The creak from the staircase told her where Neil was. The third step from the bottom. She could just make out his silhouette as he stood silently, his left foot frozen in the air. A sharp crack sounded from the parlour and Neil's shadow disappeared. Blood pounded thunderously in her ears. She paused indecisively on the staircase. Where was Neil? The parlour lights came on with a suddenness that knocked her off balance, and she clutched at the staircase railing. A scraping sound echoed from the front of the house, quickly followed by a sharp crack. Louder now. A blast of cold air swirled up the stairs and she clenched her teeth to hold back a rising scream of hysteria.

Neil appeared in the parlour doorway, grinning when he saw her clinging to the banister. 'Come on down and see your burglar,' he invited.

Her rubbery legs barely supported her down the staircase. In the parlour Neil stood in front of a window that gaped open to the blustery night, the heavy curtains swaying in the night breezes. 'He got away,' she breathed. 'Did you see him?'

'Look out of the window and see him yourself.'

Forewarned by the trace of amusement in his voice,

Tracy cautiously stuck her head through the open window. A gust of wind slapped her in the face with a burst of sharp icy crystals at the same moment that the window's loose wooden shutter banged against the wall with a sharp crack.

Neil yanked her back inside. 'I'll fix it tomorrow.' He wasn't looking at her as he shut the window with a loud scraping sound, but there was no mistaking the laughter beneath his words.

'It did sound like someone inside,' Tracy said defensively.

'I didn't say it didn't.'

'You thought so, too.'

'I admit it.'

'I wouldn't have bothered you if I hadn't been positive that it was an intruder.'

'I'm sure you wouldn't have.'

'I'm sorry I woke you.'

'I'm not complaining.'

Fortunately Neil snapped off the parlour lights with his last remark, because Tracy knew without a doubt that her face was an embarrassing shade of crimson. She marched out to the staircase and promptly stumbled over the bottom step.

Neil flipped on the hall lights. 'That better?'

'Yes, thank you.' She refused to face him.

'For me, too.'

More blood rushed to her cheeks at the barely suppressed laughter in his voice. If he said one word about what had happened upstairs. . .'Goodnight,' she said, her back rigid. 'I hope you don't have any trouble getting back to sleep.'

Neil chuckled. 'I'm sure I will—because every time I close my eyes I'm going to see that cute little bottom marching indignantly up the stairs.'

Tracy whirled, her hands automatically going behind her to shield herself. 'You're no gentleman,' she charged.

Neil unleashed a slow, sultry smile that sent twin flags of colour to her cheeks. 'That didn't bother you earlier.' He started slowly up the stairs, his gaze holding hers. 'In my bed,' he added, as if he needed to make his meaning clear.

Tracy backed up. 'You know why I was there.' Her foot fumbled behind her for the next step.

'Of course I do,' he said soothingly, his eyes glittering in the hall light.

Backing up to the next level, she stepped down on the hem of her gown and stumbled. Neil swept her up into his arms and carried her up the remainder of the staircase. Before she could protest he set her firmly down on the floor of the upper hallway. 'Thank you,' she said breathlessly. Her heart pounded. From her near fall, she told herself.

'I wanted you to know that I can be a gentleman.' His hands cupped her elbows. 'When I want.' He slid his hands slowly up her arms with a light touch that tantalised her sensitive skin. 'No matter how tough you make it.' Fingers glided across her shoulders. Thumbs made erotic forays up the sides of her neck.

'I——' She cleared her throat and tried again. 'I'd better get back to bed before I freeze to death. I-I must be covered in goose bumps.'

Neil's lips twitched. 'You could say that.'

Tracy followed the direction of his rapt gaze. The cold had chilled her nipples into tight buttons that pressed against the sheer fabric of her gown. Hastily she crossed her arms over her chest and backed away. 'Well, goodnight,' she said lamely.

Neil let her get as far as her bedroom door. 'If you hear any more mysterious noises, don't hesitate to wake me.' His wicked grin would have done credit to the devil himself. 'You do it so well.'

With the skies lightening outside, Tracy gave up trying to recapture sleep and padded on bare feet over to the window. Elbows on the chilly sill, she watched as the dawning sun outlined the eastern horizon with a fiery yellow crayon. The early-rising juncoes were already feasting below the feeders, ignoring the criss-crossing trails of rabbit tracks in the snow. Movement near the edge of the yard caught her attention. The female bluebird, beak full of building material, flew down from the roof of the birdhouse and disappeared inside. The male would leave most of the nest-building to her, but he'd be in the vicinity. As any squirrel who intruded on the female and her domestic chores would quickly find out.

The female bluebird would lay her eggs if and when she was ready, not before. The male, her protector, would not tease and torment her. Unlike some members of the human species. Tracy scowled as she watched the drab female launch from the birdhouse. Birds and animals definitely had the advantage when it came to male and female relationships. No doubts. No confusion. No outside influences. No reading significance into insignificant actions. Just do what comes naturally. The human race, on the other hand, was lucky that it managed to reproduce itself.

Not that she was interested in reproducing anything besides her miniature houses. Especially with a man like Neil Charles. He must think he was the gods' gift to women, giving that disgusting little smirk last night. In retrospect she supposed that she had looked foolish skulking through the dark night in fear of a loose wooden shutter, but then he hadn't exactly won any awards for brilliance himself. She giggled as she remembered him frozen on the step, obviously worried that the creak had betrayed him. Once Neil had discovered the source of their mysterious noise, he'd conveniently forgotten that he'd been as fooled as she had been.

The furnace switched on with a lumbering groan, reminding her that she was hardly dressed for the chill, early morning air. She glanced down. The whipped honey satin and creamy lace nightgown had been less appropriate last night. No wonder Neil had misunderstood her foray into his bed. She knew exactly what conclusion she would have reached if he'd crawled into bed and snuggled up to her wearing nothing but those vivid blue-striped briefs he'd had on last night. The memory of those briefs brought a half-smile to her face. A smile which faded instantly as Tracy recalled all too well the rippling muscles and satiny warmth of Neil's back beneath her hands. Outrageous as the briefs might have been, there had been nothing laughable about the well-shaped body wearing them.

CHAPTER SIX

THE enticing aroma of freshly ground coffee drifting down to the workshop made a mockery of the instant coffee Tracy had drunk earlier. Her stomach growled as the smell of bacon mingled with paint fumes. Neil was fixing breakfast. Hunger warred with a reluctance to face him after last night's embarrassing false alarm. She dipped her thin brush into the white paint and randomly painted light and heavy lines over the splotches of black, grey, slate-blue and white paint that she'd dabbed on the day before. Heavy footsteps pounded down the basement staircase.

'That loud enough to announce my presence?' Neil asked.

'Yes, thank you.' She concentrated on her work.

Neil peered curiously over her shoulder. 'What is it?'

'One of the fireplaces.'

'Why don't you use real marble?'

'The veining would be too large for a doll's house.'

'Incredible. It really does look like the real thing. What's this?' He picked up the small chunk of marble that lay on the workbench.

'White marble from the old quarry near Marble, Colorado. According to letters, the fireplace in the original dining-room came from there. The site is protected, but I managed to find this chunk downstream in the Crystal River. It's going to be tough to duplicate it in miniature.'

Neil rubbed the smooth surface. 'It's beautiful.'

'I know. The Lincoln Memorial in Washington, DC is made from that marble.' She stood back from the tiny fireplace and studied it through narrowed eyes. Over her shoulder she asked, 'Did you want something?'

'Actually, I thought you might. Breakfast.'

'I already ate.' If one could call a piece of toast eating.

'You must have been up with the chickens.'

'Sort of. I couldn't sleep.'

'Bad dreams about bogeymen?'

The bland voice didn't fool Tracy. 'Are you ever going to forget that I panicked at a false alarm and woke you up?'

'Oh, I expect that I'll forget about the panic sooner or later,' Neil drawled. 'It's the waking me up that I may have trouble erasing from my mind.' He wiggled his eyebrows in a lecherous leer.

'I thought it was an emergency. And you were quick enough to believe there was an intruder, too,' she pointed out.

'You're right, I did, but I just can't resist teasing you. . .the way you stiffen up and get that funny look on your face, half-way between mad and embarrassed.'

'Very amusing!' Tracy snapped.

'Sure it is,' Neil agreed, his mouth turning up at the corners. 'Think about it. You tiptoeing desperately across the hall to my room, and me tiptoeing just as desperately down the stairs.' His grin widened. 'In my underwear, no less. Wouldn't I have scared a burglar half to death?'

Tracy smiled reluctantly. 'Only if he were afraid of hairy legs.'

Neil gave a choke of laughter. '*Touché*. Now, come

on, be a good girl and have breakfast with me. Bacon and a cheese omelette,' he added in a coaxing voice.

'All right. Let me straighten up here.'

Neil waited for her, poking curiously about her workshop. 'What's this?' He held up a small wooden house that had a hole on the front side. 'A birdhouse?'

'Yes. I made it for Stan for Christmas. It was in one of the boxes you brought down from Mother's closet. I can't think how it got there.' The sight of the house produced unpleasant memories and she quickly changed the subject. 'My bluebird couple appear to have chosen the state capital again this year to nest in. That's the birdhouse with the gold dome. I built the Victorian house for them, modelling it after the Maxwell House in the old mining town of Georgetown, Colorado because I thought the pink trim would be so lovely against their blue feathers. Someone once said that the bluebird carries the blue of the sky on his back, and that's so true, don't you think?' Without waiting for an answer she nervously babbled on, ignoring the startled look on Neil's face at the onslaught of information. 'A pair of white-breasted nuthatches moved into the house before the bluebirds showed up, and they've claimed squatters' rights ever since. Some mountain chickadees have been investigating the log cabin, so I guess I'll have to put out a no-vacancy sign.' She pushed back her stool. 'There. I'm ready for breakfast.'

'Why don't I put this house up?' Neil suggested. 'Maybe another pair of bluebirds will move in.'

'No,' Tracy said sharply. At his look of surprise, she added, 'Bluebirds are territorial and two pairs won't nest in the same area.' She started out of the workshop. 'I'm starving.'

Breakfast was not the ordeal she'd feared. Neil made not a single reference to her middle-of-the-night summons, but kept the conversation firmly centred on her work. Encouraged by his interest, she expanded enthusiastically upon her future plans. One revelation led to another, and soon she was telling him about her agent and the commissions he'd lined up for her, as well as about the magazine dedicated to miniatures that had featured one of her houses on its cover.

'Very impressive,' Neil said. 'What intrigues me, however, is how you ever got into such a field.'

'I started with a doll's house I'd received as a gift. It was badly made and in constant need of repairs. Stan's handyman possessed both a shop full of tools and a great deal of patience. One thing led to another. Stan encouraged me to become an architect. I did take design and drafting courses in college, but working in miniature held more appeal. Besides, with a real house I'd have to deal with contractors, subcontractors, delivery men. . .' She grimaced. 'Doing the entire house myself means everything is done exactly how I want it.'

'Strange I'd never heard any of this before.'

Tracy shrugged. 'My friends know, but most of them consider it as "Tracy's little hobby". I guess compared to their society marriages or high-powered careers, building doll's houses doesn't have much glamour.' She fiddled with her fork. 'Talking about it too much seemed to trivialise it.' Her voice took on a high, artificial tone. 'Débutante Tracy Warner and her adorable little houses. Aren't they cute?' Returning to her normal voice, she added, 'I'm gaining a reputation in the field with the people who count, and I don't want that ruined by them reading about my work in the society pages.'

'No wonder you resented my crack about you dabbling in the art world.'

'"Artsy-crafty", I believe you said.'

Neil laughed. 'Do you remember everything I said to you?'

'On that day, yes, I guess I pretty much do. The possibility of proving Stan's innocence, Mother's will, the demands, everything was so unexpected that it's burned into my memory.' She hesitated. 'You said a lot of things about me that day that were no more true than what you said about my work.'

'Did I?'

She concentrated on tearing her paper napkin into long strips. 'Do you still believe everything you said?'

'I don't share your phenomenal recall. Refresh my memory.'

There was only the barest tremor in her voice as she said, 'You called me a typical rich, spoiled brat.'

'I must have been out of my mind.' She looked sharply at him, mustrusting the amusement in his voice. 'There isn't anything the slightest bit typical about you.' He leaned across the table and covered her hand with his. 'I do recall that I also said you were beautiful. That's certainly true.'

Tracy could feel the soft colour stealing over her cheeks. 'You were very determined to dislike me.' The words were half challenge and half plea for reassurance. She felt his withdrawal even before he lifted his hand from hers.

'I thought the conditions of our truce were based on ignoring our pasts.'

She should have left well enough alone, instead of pressing Neil to acknowledge that he'd been wrong about her. Wanting more from a person than that person was willing to give was always dangerous. 'Well,' she forced gaiety into her voice, 'I suppose a lawyer can't make a judgement until the evidence is all in.'

A shadow passed over his face. 'That wouldn't be a bad policy for you to follow, either. People aren't always what they seem at first.' Out in the hall the phone rang and Neil went to answer it.

Leaving Tracy to puzzle over his words. There had been an odd inflection in his voice. Was he warning her that the villain was going to turn out to be someone she knew and liked? Or was he reminding her that she had judged Jake Archer without knowing all the facts? He was a fine one to talk. Whatever had happened to innocent until proven guilty? She tried to swallow her irritation. It was her fault for stepping over the boundary of their truce. She mustn't forget that their armistice was only temporary. Once the murder was solved. . .Lost in her thoughts, she didn't hear Neil come back, and his tap on her shoulder caught her by surprise. She blinked up at him. 'What?'

He jerked his thumb towards the hall. 'Jess is on the phone.'

'Ed just told me,' Jess said immediately. 'I couldn't believe it. I thought all this bodyguard business was just a lot of nonsense. Thank goodness you followed Neil,' she added, clearing up Tracy's confusion.

'How did you know?'

'Neil called Ed this morning after he'd called the police and your father.'

Tracy hadn't realised Neil had been so busy. It was strange that he hadn't mentioned the calls to her. Was it because he wanted to downplay what had happened, or because he didn't want to admit that Jake hadn't been interested?

'. . .and I said of course it wouldn't be, but Ed simply wouldn't listen,' Jess said.

Tracy dragged her attention back to Jess's conversation. 'What wouldn't be?'

'Having you here.' Her impatience came clearly over the wires. 'I want you to stay with us until this mess is cleared up, but Ed insists that it's too much trouble for me.'

Tracy shook her head as if to clear away the fog. 'Ed doesn't want me to come?' she repeated.

'Men!' Jess stormed. 'He doesn't care about you,' she added cruelly. 'It's me he wants to strike back at.'

Tracy was immediately side-tracked from her own problems by the pain in Jess's voice. 'What's the matter? Did you and Ed have a fight?'

'Certainly not,' Jess said with outraged dignity. 'Ed is just being childish. One minute he accuses me of spoiling the twins and picking them up the instant they cry, and the next he's yelling at me because I don't spend enough time with them. Could I help it if I had to stay home from the dinner-party last night because Cathy is cutting a tooth? Is it my fault I got roped into doing that big charity fashion show again this spring? I'm only supposed to be the co-chairman, but I've done it for the last two years so everyone leaves everything to me.' There was the unmistakable sound of a sob. 'I've been so busy and so tired, and now with Ed harassing me. . .I don't know why I ever married him. . .' Once launched, Jess was not to be dissuaded from cataloguing every sin that Ed had committed from the day they'd met each other to the present. Tracy, accustomed to the role of Jess's confidante, settled down to listen.

When she returned to the kitchen, Neil was tidying up. 'Problems at the Baldwins'?' he asked as he handed her a towel.

Tracy picked up a dripping plate. 'Nothing that couldn't be worked out if Ed would grow up a little.'

Neil gave her a quizzical look. 'It takes two to tango.'

'Not in this case. Ed is behaving like a jerk. Here's poor Jess with twins, and Ed not only does nothing to help her out, he gets furious when she won't drop whatever she's doing so that she can entertain him.'

'Correct me if I'm wrong, but don't the Baldwins have a nanny as well as a housekeeper?'

'I suppose you think that it's perfectly acceptable for the housekeeper to take the girls to the dentist, or the gardener to drive them to dancing lessons. And when there's an event at school that they want their mother to attend, she can try to buy them off with new dresses because she's going somewhere more important with their father.' Suddenly she was conscious that, in her eagerness to convince him, she had revealed too much.

'We're not talking about the Baldwin twins, are we?' Neil asked slowly.

'Of course we are.'

Neil ignored her breathless avowal. 'I always pictured you as a spoiled little kid with a mother, a stepfather and a million servants, each waiting breathlessly to grant your every wish. But what you just said, that was your life, wasn't it? Now I understand the remark you made earlier about Stan Warner being just your stepfather. I suppose he resented having to raise another man's kid.'

'No, it wasn't like that at all,' Tracy denied. 'I thought so at first, and blamed him for stealing away my mother, but I was wrong.' Automatically she accepted the damp glass that Neil handed her. 'I loved my mother, but she wasn't a strong person,' she admitted. 'My grandparents used to tell me how obedient my mother was as a child. I think the only time she ever defied their wishes was when she married Jake Archer. And time proved that they were right and she was wrong. You have to understand that she was raised in an era that insisted a woman's most important role in life was to be a successful wife.'

'Other women manage to be both wife and mother.'

'Stronger women. Stan petted and pampered Mother, and in return she focused all her thoughts and energies on pleasing him. She'd failed with Jake; she wouldn't be left again.'

'And to hell with her kid.'

'If necessary.' Tracy took a deep breath and put the glass in the cupboard. 'Anyway, I survived, and I learned a very valuable lesson in the process. I don't depend on anybody except Tracy Warner. I am never going to need another person the way my mother did.' Neil handed her another wet plate and they worked in silence for a few moments. It seemed to Tracy that her last words hung defiantly in the air between them.

'It's one thing to expect someone else to hold the entire responsibility for your happiness in their hands,' Neil finally said, 'and quite another to occasionally lean on someone else.'

Tracy shook her head. 'And if that someone isn't

there when you'd like to lean on them? What happens then? You fall smack on your face. It's much easier to never count on them at all.'

'Most people have moments when they feel weak and vulnerable. Husbands and wives, for example.'

Tracy rolled her eyes. 'Now you're an expert on marriage.'

'I don't claim to be an expert,' Neil said, 'but I do have eyes in my head. You said yourself that having twins has caused an upheaval in Jess's life. Don't you think the same is true of Ed? Every time I've been around the Baldwins, Jessica was totally absorbed with the twins while poor Ed hovered around the fringes looking totally neglected and lonely. How do you think he feels having awakened one morning to discover that his lover and companion had turned into the mother of his children?'

'I never looked at it that way,' Tracy admitted. She looked at Neil curiously. 'Do you deal with a lot of divorces?'

'Not if I can help it. Unless there's something involved like wife-beating or child-abuse, I counsel my clients to seek outside help. Marriage is tough, but if both partners are committed to making it work, then they will seek solutions to their problems. If there's no commitment, then it's disposable like paper napkins. Toss it in the trash and try again. Only they'll go on making the same mistakes.' He draped his damp teatowel over Tracy's shoulder. 'That's the last of the dishes. Why don't you phone Jess and make a date for the four of us to go out to dinner next weekend? Tell her that the waiting is getting on your nerves. Ed won't have her alone, but at least the twins won't be along.'

* * *

Jess had been amazingly amenable to Tracy's suggestion that the four of them go out to dinner. A spicy odour from the kitchen invaded the basement workshop, making Tracy's mouth water. The restaurant was going to find it difficult to serve a meal better than Neil's creations. Her stomach was going to miss him. As was her house. Despite his earlier demands that Tracy share the chores, he had taken over the house-cleaning duties with a vengeance. Her furniture and windows had never known such a gleam. When she'd objected Neil had welcomed the opportunity to embarrass her by pointing out that she was the one who had said that he may as well be useful. After he'd enjoyed her discomfort, he'd claimed he needed to do something to occupy his time. There were times when Tracy wondered if Neil were motivated less by boredom and more by the knowledge that she needed to spend almost every waking minute in her workshop in order to meet her advancing deadline. A theory she dared not expose to Neil's ridicule.

Tracy had been able to view Neil more objectively once she had agreed to his suggestion that they suspend hostilities. When he banged pots and pans around in the kitchen she realised that he was merely clumsy, instead of immediately concluding that he resented doing the cooking. When he sang slightly naughty songs in the shower every morning, her first thought was that he was flat, not that he was trying to disconcert her. In fact, Neil was rather a pleasant companion. Heaven knew they still argued, but over neutral topics. The existence of Jake Archer and her relationship to him were strictly forbidden territory. By tacit agreement, no mention was made of the physical attraction that existed between them either.

Purely chemical, of course, Tracy told herself. Nothing more than spring fever.

Supper was almost ready when she came up from the basement.

'You're going to spoil me,' she said, lifting a lid and breathing deeply of the spicy spaghetti sauce.

'Or fatten you up.' He indicated the garlic bread dripping with butter on the table.

'Are you saying I'm skinny?'

'Quit digging for a compliment. Don't you have a mirror in your bedroom?'

'Of course I do. A beautiful old cheval one that used to belong to my grandmother. So?' He looked expectantly at her. 'Oh,' she said, comprehension and pleasure arriving together at his indirect reference to the fact that if she had a mirror she must know how good she looked. 'Thank you. I think.'

'You're welcome. I think,' he mimicked. 'You were so slow on the uptake, I was afraid I'd been too subtle for you.'

'It's just that you're the last person I'd expect subtlety from,' she retorted.

He stirred the sauce and eyed her with interest. 'Why?'

'Because a line like "Creamy shoulders that beg for a man's lips" is hardly a subtle masterpiece.'

'Hits you right between the eyes, doesn't it?'

'Definitely.'

'But all the same. . .' Taking the wooden spoon from the large pot, he took a lick of the sauce which coated it. 'You didn't forget it.'

'I haven't forgotten the last time I went to the dentist, either,' she countered tartly.

'He another boyfriend?' Neil asked with spurious interest.

'No. He sticks needles in my mouth and drills holes in my teeth. The level of pleasure ranks right up there with dancing with you.'

'Liar,' he said pleasantly, setting the spoon on the cabinet and dampening a paper towel. 'Come here.'

'Why?' She started to back away.

He was too quick for her. A long arm brought her up short and pulled her to stand between his legs as he leaned against the counter. 'There's a smudge on your nose.'

'I can wash it,' she said hastily. To her surprise, he handed her the damp towel. A second later she realised why he'd been so agreeable. Both his hands were now free to wrap around her body. Ignoring them and the way her pulse speeded up, she scrubbed at her nose. 'Did I get it?' A large hand held her face for his inspection as he leaned closer. 'Near-sighted?'

Neil sighed. 'Merely blinded by your beauty.'

It was such an outrageous remark that Tracy would have roared with laughter—if she could have. The kitchen was redolent with the pungent fragrance of spaghetti. Little bubbles of sound came from a pot of boiling water, the bubbles popping faster and faster in rhythm with Tracy's beating heart. The kitchen was warm, unbearably warm. Neil's long legs penned her against his hips, his hands burned her back. She closed her eyes to block out the dangerous flames in his.

'Damn!'

Tracy's eyes shot open as Neil pushed her away. Reaching over to the stove, he grabbed the large pan and quickly moved it to another burner.

'You made me burn the spaghetti sauce,' he complained.

Tracy stared speechlessly at him as he stirred the tomato-red mixture, a scorched odour rising from the pan. 'I made you!' she said, finding her voice at last. '*I* made you!' Without waiting for an answer, she flounced from the kitchen.

Standing beneath the hot shower, Tracy belatedly thought of all the witty remarks she could have made in the kitchen instead of tearing from the room. Stepping from the shower, she briskly towelled off her body. Neil probably thought that she was upset because he didn't kiss her. She jerked a comb through her wet, tangled hair and threw on some clothes. She'd explain her rush by saying she'd spilled turpentine on her arms and had been in an urgent need of a shower. Neil might even believe her.

He was standing in the hallway when she came down. 'I'm sorry to say that my great spaghetti sauce was a total loss.'

'I'm not surprised. Such an inattentive cook,' she said carelessly, proud of the way her voice kept her secrets.

He grinned at her. 'Dinner out can be my treat.'

Grabbing her coat from the stand in the hall, Tracy jammed her arms in the sleeves. 'You talked me into it.'

'I thought you were a liberated woman,' he said. 'Aren't you ever going to offer to buy your own dinner?'

'Nope. You burned the spaghetti.' Closing the door, she started off down the street.

'That was your fault,' Neil said, ambling along at her side. 'Aren't we taking the car?'

'No. You need the exercise. And it was not my fault.'

'Sure it was. You distracted the cook.'

'Distracted the cook! All I did was walk into the room.'

'I suppose you're going to deny that you had a provocative smudge on your cute little nose.'

There was no answer to that. Tracy plunged ahead down the hill. His long legs easily matched her stride. The sun set early so close to the western foothills, and the evening air was already chilled. A door was open somewhere, and the voices of the evening newscasters ebbed and flowed with the breeze. A couple of daffodils lay along the kerb, flattened by the snow and winds of Thursday evening.

'Why do I need the exercise?' Neil referred to her earlier comment.

'To get rid of some of your excess energy.' Tracy schooled her face to remain perfectly sober. 'Or you could try the remedy they used to use in my grandmother's day. A dose of salts.'

Neil was still chuckling when they reached the small restaurant. A sleek sports car turned off the main street and pulled to a stop in the restaurant car park. The driver rolled down his window. 'This is a pleasant surprise.'

The sour look on Neil's face immediately told Tracy that Blake Campbell's unexpected appearance wasn't a pleasant surprise to Neil. She spoke up hastily before he could make the hostile remark that she could almost see dripping from the tip of his tongue. 'Blake. What are you doing in Palmer Lake?'

'I had some business in Colorado Springs this afternoon, so I thought I'd drop by and see how you were getting along.'

'How kind of you. As a matter of fact, we were just on our way to eat here.' She shot Neil a look of appeal. Surely he would see that she had no choice. 'Why don't you——?'

'Join us,' Neil's deep baritone finished her sentence.

She gave him a smile of appreciation.

'Thanks. I'd like that.' Taking Tracy's arm, Blake guided her towards the entrance. Neil immediately pre-empted her other arm. Tracy had the strangest feeling that the two men were indulging in some strange male ritual, and that she had been chosen to play a minor role—that of the sacrificial victim. A strange and powerful urge to run screaming from the restaurant swept through her body. Instead, she meekly followed the hostess through the bar to their pink-cloth-covered table.

Their order given, Blake picked up his wine glass and drank deeply, studying Tracy over the glass's rim. 'How are you doing? I worry about you.'

'No need for that.' Neil beat her to the answer. 'Tracy's tough. Besides,' he leaned back and casually draped his arm over the back of her chair, 'I'm here.'

Blake raised one eyebrow an eighth of an inch. 'But for how long?'

Neil's hand moved to massage her back. 'As long as she needs me.' There was the subtlest emphasis on the word 'needs'.

'How are things at the plant?' Tracy quickly asked.

'Messy.' Blake gave her a fleeting glance. 'Stan must have been mentally ill to do what he did.'

'He didn't. . .' Tears sprang to her eyes at the sudden pain.

'Didn't what?' Blake asked sharply.

'He didn't know what he was doing,' Neil explained. 'He couldn't have. Mental illness is as good an explanation as any, wouldn't you agree, Tracy?'

She nodded. If she didn't, Neil was quite capable of kicking her again. Glaring at him, she rubbed her right ankle with her left. Across the room a table of four discussed the disgrace and humiliation of a friend who'd been charged with shoplifting. From the bar came a sudden burst of laughter.

Blake refilled Tracy's wine glass. 'I don't know how we all missed it. Didn't you notice anything different about him?'

She shook her head. 'Nothing.'

'Are you sure? There must have been hints, indications. Think,' Blake urged. 'You must have suspected something.'

Tracy stared at him. 'Why must I?' she asked slowly, her curiositiy aroused by his persistent questioning. Neil stirred at her side and she quickly moved her legs out of his range.

Blake gave her a crooked smile, the hard lines of his face dissolving and reforming into his normal charming, boyish looks. 'I don't mean to sound so impassioned. I guess I feel a little guilty about what happened. Looking back on it, I wonder about things that seemed insignificant at the time.'

'Such as?' Neil asked, his hand etching large circles on Tracy's back.

'He was acting mysterious, secretive, paranoid. I tried to get him to talk about it, but. . .' Blake shrugged. 'Have you gone through the boxes you picked up the other day?'

'No,' Tracy said. 'They're just filled with my school memorabilia, yearbooks, stuff like that. Nothing valuable.'

'I thought perhaps. . .whatever was on Stan's mind, he said he wanted to discuss it with you.'

'Me?' Tracy asked in astonishment.

'Stan thought a lot of you,' Blake said. 'He was proud of your accomplishments. He must have told me a thousand times that you'd inherited your real father's brains. I know the two of you were very close.'

Tracy's startled gaze met Neil's amused one. Blake's comment certainly shattered her conviction that his lack of interest in her was based on a belief that she didn't count with her stepfather. Blake turned to speak to the waiter and Neil leaned closer to Tracy, his breath disturbing tendrils of her hair. 'Apparently you just didn't turn him on.'

'What are you two lovebirds whispering about?' Blake asked.

Tracy felt the hot blush that coloured her cheeks, but Neil was made of sterner stuff. 'Lovers' talk,' he said, his hand moving up to caress the back of her neck. 'All this discussion about the tragedy upsets Tracy. I thought it was time to turn her thoughts to a more pleasant subject.' The sleepy-eyed, sultry expression on his face left no doubt as to what he considered more pleasant. Tracy's colour deepened.

Blake was instantly apologetic. 'I've been thoughtless.'

The only one not mortified was Neil. Tracy shot him a scathing look that promised retribution, and then quickly guided the conversation on to neutral topics. Neil grinned unrepentantly before supporting her efforts, but Blake was obviously restive and anxious to escape from them.

And escape he did, driving off alone towards

Denver, leaving Neil and Tracy standing in the car park.

Tracy shivered and gathered her coat close around her. 'Brrr. It's cold out tonight. If you hadn't acted like a rutting stag, he'd at least have driven us home.'

Neil laughed, unfazed by her cutting remark. 'If you hadn't turned such a lovely shade of guilty scarlet, his mind wouldn't have immediately leaped to the conclusion that I was referring to sex. As yours did,' he added shamelessly.

'If you mean to tell me that wasn't your intent. . .'

'No, I don't.' Neil tucked her hand into the curve of his arm. 'It's too lovely a night to waste arguing.'

'Don't you mean that you need to save your breath to get yourself uphill?'

'That's what I like about you. Your sensitivity to the male ego. Most women would have unobtrusively slowed down. Few would have been crude enough to point out that my lungs are about to burst from the unfamiliar altitude, and that my heart is going to give out at any minute.'

Tracy laughed. Neil was hardly breathing heavily. Still, she slowed down her pace. There was a sharp bite to the night air, but they were dressed warmly so there was no need to indulge in a foot race up the hill. The stars were bright pinpoints of light in the cloudless sky, and Tracy picked out the Big Dipper with ease. Below them a warning whistle announced the passage of a coal-train through town.

'It's odd when you think about it. That a sophisticate with a ladies' man reputation would be so uncomfortable with what, after all, was a very nebulous reference.'

Tracy looked up. In the dark Neil's face was a

composite of shadowed planes and mysterious angles. 'It was obvious to me.'

Neil squeezed her arm against his side. 'That's because you can't put my nice legs out of your mind.'

'Speaking of legs, what was the idea of kicking mine?'

'I couldn't have you giving away our little plot. We don't want Blake thinking that we don't believe Stan committed those crimes.' Neil glanced down at her. 'I suspect that Blake is doing a little kicking himself right now.' Inside the house, he helped her off with her coat.

'Because he feels guilty about what happened, you mean? If he knew the truth, then. . .'

'Because, my dear Tracy, the thought of me in your bed suddenly pointed out to him that's where he'd like to be.'

'That's ridiculous.' She moved into the front parlour.

'Why?' Neil sprawled out on the sofa and propped his long legs up on a fat ottoman. 'Any man who thinks that you and your stepfather were "very close".' He mimicked perfectly Blake's voice. 'That ought to establish that he's not too bright.'

'Meaning only a dummy would want to sleep with me.'

'You ought to know better than me the type of men who normally slip between your sheets.' His eyes were closed, his lashes indecently dark and long against his lightly tanned face.

'The non-existent type!' After a chagrined pause, she added belatedly, 'Not that it's any of your business.'

One eyelid opened a crack. 'Non-existent? As in

never? A beautiful woman like you? Why not? Too particular?'

'No. Frigid,' she snapped.

Neil uttered a short laugh. 'That we both know you're not.'

'I don't know how we got on to this stupid conversation anyway. If Blake is kicking himself about anything, it's that he somehow feels that he should have been able to stop what happened.' She shivered. 'I'll be glad when it's over and done with, so Mother and Stan can rest in peace.' Her throat tightened. 'I wonder if Stan really was going to confide in me. Now that I've grown up, well, I'd started appreciating him for what he was, not what I wanted him to be. We were becoming friends of a sort. Maybe if I'd tried harder. . .'

'Don't waste your time thinking about something you can't change,' Neil advised. 'Blake was in a better position than you to help Stan out, and he couldn't. He's probably just trying to get you to share his guilt.'

'That's a cynical thing to say.'

'He professes to be concerned about you, yet all he managed to do at dinner was upset you. Forget Blake and his problems. Forget the bad memories and concentrate on good thoughts. Tell me what makes you feel good.'

'What a strange request.' But she answered it, one hand on the arm of her chair propping up her chin. 'Spring. The first pasque-flower of the season. The bluebirds returning. Baby fawns still wearing their spots. Jess's twins just out of the bathtub. Softly falling snow.' She thought for a minute. 'A hillside covered with golden aspen in the fall. Tulips and crocuses and daffodils and lilacs. *Singing in the Rain*.

The movie, I mean. Now it's your turn. What makes you feel good?'

'Hearing you laugh,' he said lazily, his eyes closed.

'That's cheating,' Tracy charged. 'You just said that so I'd be embarrassed and change the subject. Well, I'm not going to let you get off that easy. Play fair and take your turn.'

'The Statue of Liberty, lovers in Central Park, ice-skaters at the Rockefeller Center, a new snow before traffic turns it into dirty muck, a good book, an excellent meal, fine wine, good friends, interesting conversation.' He reeled off the entire list without taking a breath. Tracy laughed. 'And. . .' a pause gave quiet emphasis to his next words '. . .hearing you laugh.'

She considered him as he sprawled lazily on the sofa, eyes closed, arms crossed over his stomach. Even half asleep he was six feet of potent masculinity. No wonder his kisses made her head spin. She curled her feet beneath her in the large chair. He had a strong face and a firm jawline that bespoke a man who would not be pushed around. The self-assurance which, at times, gave birth to a shocking arrogance also produced a quiet confidence which would induce others to rely on him in times of trouble. As Jake Archer had.

'Made up your mind?'

'About what?'

'Me.'

'What makes you so sure that I'm thinking about you? Conceited, aren't you?'

'No. But then I'm not blind like you are, either.'

CHAPTER SEVEN

SURREPTITIOUSLY Tracy studied Neil as they drove up to Denver several days later. She knew exactly what he had been alluding to the other night. She'd simply chosen to ignore it. If one *could* ignore a current of sexual tension as strong as the one that had vibrated between the two of them. The air between them had practically snapped and sizzled. Tracy tried to convince herself that her heightened sensibilities had nothing to do with Neil and everything to do with the stressful situation in which she found herself.

'To a city boy, this scenery is on the spooky side. When I think of Colorado, I think of mountains and waterfalls and lakes. This looks like no man's land.'

Tracy looked around at the dull landscape as they headed north on I25. 'The mountains are there to the west.' The heavy snowpack on the slate-blue peaks was a chilly reminder that spring was slow in coming to the Rockies this year. Even the sky was leaden and lifeless today. Patches of snow decorated the giant buttes that rose from the land, and the willows that grew along the sluggish stream-bed were brown and stark against the washed-out sky.

It was as if Mother Nature was holding her breath with the willows, waiting for the proper moment to burst forth with their spring finery. Bird nests, easily seen in the leafless trees, were abandoned now, but soon mating pairs would seek them out. Three large black crows flapped into flight from their perch on the telephone wires that paralleled the road, and a small flock of blackbirds rose abruptly from a large old tree that leaned drunkenly towards the land. A shadow moved over the car, a small hawk after his dinner.

Neil glanced over at her. 'I like that outfit you're wearing. With that fancy blouse, ruffled skirt and boots, you look like a genuine cowgirl.'

'I can assure you that this outfit was never meant to get anywhere near a horse. Speaking of clothes, I appreciate your helping me with this before we go out to dinner. Jess's church has a clothing drive for the poor every spring, and I have to go through the clothing some time. We'll have to stop by Jess's and ask her where she wants me to take everything.'

'Her place isn't that far out of our way,' Neil said.

Jess met them at the door. 'Oh, no! I was going to call and cancel our dinner plans. Why are you here so early?'

Tracy explained about the clothes, unable to drag her eyes from her normally exquisitely attired friend. Jess was wearing a bedraggled, food-stained dress, with something green that resembled mashed peas in her hair and trying in vain to hush the crying twin that rode on her hip. 'What's wrong?' Tracy stepped into the white-panelled foyer and automatically reached for the baby.

'Everything!' Jess cried dramatically. 'Nanny left last night to go to a friend's wedding, and I told her not to come back until tomorrow because I thought that the housekeeper and I could handle the girls ourselves for two days, but then her sister had to go and have a heart attack and naturally I told her to go ahead and fly out to California, and then Ed said that he had to make an unexpected trip to New York and he'll be gone for a couple of days and he wanted me to come along, and how could I possibly go?' She burst into tears. A sound that was immediately echoed by a wail from the back of the house. 'Candy!' Jess said and dashed off.

Neil loosened his tie. 'I don't like the look on your face.'

Tracy handed him the baby and followed Jess.

'Ed is furious with me because I wouldn't go with him, but what would I do with the twins? Ed's mother would stay with them, but she has the flu,' Jess sniffed, her tear-stained face looking remarkably like her daughters'.

Tracy looked at Neil, who'd followed them into the sunny family-room. He was patiently watching the twin in his arms try to make a meal of his red tie. Expensive Italian silk, Tracy thought guiltily as she recalled what Jess had said about Cathy cutting a tooth. Neil intercepted her look of appeal. Looking from his soggy tie to Jess's red-rimmed eyes, he sighed. 'Why not?' he said in resignation.

Tracy plucked Candy from the play-pen. 'Your baby-sitters have just arrived. You go and pack for a trip to New York.'

Of course, it wasn't that easy. The next hour was total pandemonium. Convincing Jess to leave her precious babies in the hands of two neophytes was only one of the obstacles that Tracy had to overcome, but at last Neil was on his way to the airport, a reluctant Jess in tow.

Tracy collapsed on the sofa. The twins were napping, looking like two apple-cheeked cherubs, their chubby arms and legs temporarily at rest. She ought to clean up the mess in the kitchen. Kicking off her shoes, Tracy lay back on the sofa. She'd close her eyes for just a minute.

A warm kiss awakened her. Neil was bending over the sofa, minus his tie, with his shirt unbuttoned at the neck. 'You've mixed up your roles,' he said.

Tracy averted her gaze from hazel eyes brimming with amusement. 'What roles are those?'

'You're supposed to be Cinderella cleaning the house, not Sleeping Beauty waiting for the handsome prince to awaken her.' He dropped to the sofa beside her.

Tracy sat up. 'And you had to ruin everything by waking me before the prince got here,' she complained. Ducking a mock punch, she asked, 'Jess get off OK?'

'Barely. She was so busy giving me last-minute instructions, I practically had to carry her to the plane.' He pulled a small notebook from his pocket. 'I'm sure she already gave you the number of her paediatrician, but I wrote it down again. And the number of every neighbour within a hundred miles, Ed's mother's number, and even the number of her mother—who's in Florida and what good she'd be. . .I solemnly promised that we will not allow the children to fall asleep with bottles in their mouths, that we will dress them warmly if we take them outside, that we will not take our eyes off them for one second, that we will call the doctor if either of the darlings so much as coughs, that we will not yell at them or slug them, and that when we put them to bed we will tell them that their mother adores them. I swore to call her if anything at all came up.' He gave Tracy a whimsical look. 'Do you suppose that last included their dinner?'

Tracy shuddered. 'Please. Don't ask for trouble.'

He grinned. 'In addition, at the last minute Jess remembered that she'd run into Blake Campbell the other day, and invited him and a date to join us for dinner tonight. You can have the privilege of cancelling that.'

'Why do you suppose she invited Blake?'

He shrugged. 'She acted rather funny about it.'

'Matchmaking,' Tracy said in disgust. 'Lives there a married woman who doesn't want to share the misery?'

'I didn't realise that you were a female version of a misogynist.'

'I'm not.'

'Prove it.'

'I don't. . .'

A finger pressed lightly against her lips silenced her. She dropped her eyes before the warm light in his, and her gaze was caught by the lightly tanned column of skin exposed by his open collar. An urge to press her lips against the small pulse beating at the base of his neck was barely suppressed. In the background, the weatherman on the radio was droning on and on about a new front rapidly moving into the Front Range, while the sharp, acrid fragrance of daffodils from the bouquet on the coffee-table assaulted her nostrils. Neil's hands slid through her hair and positioned her head to bring her lips within range of his. The kiss began as a warm and gentle caress, but Neil quickly deepened it. Tracy parted her lips at his persuasion, intent on savouring every nuance of his mouth. But when he began to unbutton her blouse, she placed a hand over his to stop him. 'This isn't a good idea,' she said.

Neil sighed. 'It seemed like it at the time, but no doubt you are right.' Just then the loud cries of a child sounded. 'Besides,' Neil said, a wry expression of resignation twisting his lips, 'duty calls.' Upstairs a second twin added her voice to the growing chorus of impatient cries.

The girls were wet, hungry and wanted to be out of bed.

'How in the world do you tell them apart?' Neil asked, as he valiantly dealt with a dirty nappy.

'Easy,' Tracy answered. 'Candy is older by a few minutes.'

'Thanks a lot. That's helpful to know.'

Tracy laughed as she swung Cathy out of her crib. 'Now that I've got to know them, it's a piece of cake. But here's a little clue for the less observant. See this little beauty mark that Cathy has on her chin? It's on the right side. Candy has the same mark, but hers is on the left side.'

'Sharp eyes, Sherlock,' Neil said in admiration.

'Thank you, Dr Watson. Er—do you mind if I point out that Candy's nappy is on inside out?'

Changing nappies turned out to be only the first of the childcare techniques in which Neil was lacking experience and, since Tracy's own limited knowledge of children came from playing with the twins and then handing them over to their nanny to have their needs met, taking care of the two lively babies who seemed to have nothing but mischief on their minds could have been an unmitigated disaster. Surprisingly, it was Neil's patience and sense of humour that prevented many an imminent tragedy. The twins promptly fell in love with him. Tracy watched in awe as he lay on the floor enduring the squirming bodies that giggled as they crawled over his chest and squealed with delight when Neil opened his eyes and said 'Boo'. His once pristine blue pin-striped shirt sported yellowish stains, and Tracy suspected that the bulge in the pocket was a cracker secreted there by Candy during snack time.

'You're awfully good with them,' Tracy said.

Neil grinned. 'It just goes to show that women of all ages are putty in my hands,' he boasted.

'I don't know about putty in your hands, but I do think there's cracker in your hair.'

'Oof.' Neil fended off the small body bouncing on his stomach. 'By the way, you didn't say what Blake had to say about our dinner being cancelled. Was he inconsolable?'

'Not noticeably. I told him that Jess and Ed had to leave town unexpectedly and that we were staying with the children.'

'Did he offer to rush right over and help us?'

'No.'

'Too bad. We could have assigned him nappy detail.'

'I have trouble visualising Blake changing dirty nappies.'

'Yesterday I would have said the same thing about me,' Neil retorted.

Tracy laughed. 'But you're doing so well.'

'Sure. Make fun of me. But, if you'll remember, I'm the one who figured out how to put the liners in those weird bottles so the girls could have their juice.'

'Well, who ever saw a baby bottle like that?' Tracy asked.

'Neither one of us,' Neil agreed. 'If Jess could see half of what's going on here today, she'd be on her way back already. We'd better hope she doesn't have second sight.'

A hope that Tracy heartily concurred with as suppertime found her practically in tears trying to get the girls to eat their vegetables. Neil took one taste of the spinach she'd opened and promptly tossed it down the drain. Her indignation was not lessened by his opening carrots which he and the girls all enjoyed. However, even Neil was appalled by the amount of carrots that ended up outside the girls.

'You know, this idea of yours was pretty clever,' Tracy admitted, looking around the bathroom.

'That's not what you said when I first suggested it,' Neil said. 'In fact, I think the word you used was "stupid".' Making loud aeroplane noises, he 'flew' a spoonful of fruit into Candy's open mouth. Cathy banged on the tray of her high-chair, yelling in her own particular language for Neil to hurry up and get to her. Both twins were stark naked as they sat strapped in their high chairs, the chairs setting squarely in the middle of Jess's enormous sunken, tiled tub. Squished beneath Neil's bare feet were nasty bits of food, and the tub was decorated with splashes of green spinach, orange carrot, creamy apple sauce and red spaghetti sauce. 'There.' Neil gave a final flourish with the spoon and said, 'All gone.' Slapping their trays, the girls uttered something undecipherable. 'Just what I thought,' Neil said. 'They want a bath.'

Tracy gurgled with laughter. 'So do you.' Neil's clothes would never be the same.

'Is their bath water ready?' he asked. At her nod he plonked a food-smeared twin in her arms. 'That will teach you to make fun of other people's appearances,' he said smoothly.

Tracy was too busy fending off Candy's enthusiastic embrace to answer.

If dinnertime was hectic, bathtime was chaotic.

Tracy's efforts to clean faces and scrub backs were seriously undermined by Neil's playing *Jaws* with a rubber duck. It was a wonder that the neighbours didn't call the police to come and investigate all the wild shrieking that came from the bathroom.

Two hours later, Neil was still trying to convince her that she'd enjoyed the bath hour as much as the rest of them had.

'The only part I agree with is that it took an hour,' she said firmly.

'You're just jealous because the rubber ducky didn't kiss you.'

'That must be it,' she said sarcastically.

'C'mon. Admit it. Bathtime was fun.'

'Easy for you to say. You didn't slip on the bar of soap that Cathy threw out of the bath.'

'How is your elbow? Want me to kiss it better?'

'No.'

Neil laughed. 'I had the distinct feeling that Candy was trying to tell you that seven p.m. is not their usual bedtime. Didn't they seem awfully wide awake to you?'

'I was too tired to notice. Nanny must be worth her weight in gold. I had no idea what caring for children involved. And two of them! No wonder Jess has felt overwhelmed by it all.'

'Didn't you ever baby-sit as a child?'

'Nope. Jess's twins are the first children I've been around. I used to think I was deprived. Today cured me of that idea.'

'Who would have thought that a kid could move that fast on all fours?'

Tracy nodded in heartfelt agreement. 'I just hope that figurine wasn't one of Jess's favourites.'

Neil grinned. 'I'm just glad that they can't talk. If

they could tell their parents about what went on here today. . .'

'At least we survived. Now all we have to do is make it through tomorrow.' A horrible thought struck her. 'I suppose that they sleep all night?'

Neil looked at her. 'How would I know?'

Tracy began to giggle helplessly. 'I'll flip you for who gets Nanny's bed next to the nursery.'

'I don't suppose that now is the time to suggest that we share it?' Neil wiggled his eyebrows.

Before Tracy could reply they heard the sound of a key turning in the front door lock. Her startled look met Neil's. Just then the phone rang.

'You get the phone. I'll check the door,' Neil said.

Tracy barely had the receiver to her ear before Jess started pouring out her woes. 'He isn't here. Ed's disappeared. He checked in as soon as he reached New York, and then he left almost immediately for a meeting. And he never came back. I've been waiting and waiting and waiting. His clothes are here and everything. He never checked out or called the hotel or anything. I'm worried, Tracy. Where can he be?'

Tracy looked over her shoulder in the direction of the front door. 'Er. . .would you believe, standing right here?'

Tracy started laughing as soon as they pulled out of the Baldwins' driveway. 'I'll never forget the look on Ed's face when he discovered that Jess was back in New York waiting for him in his hotel room.'

Neil chuckled. 'I know. He drops everything to come flying home to apologise, only to find she's gone there.' After a pause, he added, 'Let's hope it shakes them up enough so that they see what they have and how close they've come to throwing it away.'

'And if you ever decide to give up lawyering, you can always become a marriage counsellor.'

Neil glanced over at her. 'Look who's talking. You're positively diabolical. Not for one minute do I believe that you suddenly remembered you had left your curling iron plugged in.'

'As long as Ed believed it, that's all that matters.'

'He may have believed you tonight, but when he's in the middle of feeding those two little charmers of his their breakfast tomorrow morning, I'll bet he starts having his doubts. Why did we abandon Ed to his fate?'

'Abandon him? To his fate? Pardon me, but aren't those *his* children we left him with?'

'That's what I thought. Teaching Ed a lesson, are you? I wondered when you told him that you had no idea of how to reach Nanny, knowing perfectly well that Jess left Nanny's phone number in case of emergency.'

'Every father should get to know his children,' Tracy said virtuously.

'And maybe come to a better understanding of what their mother has to deal with?'

'Now why didn't I think of that?' Tracy marvelled.

'Why didn't you think of it later? After we'd had dinner? Were you afraid if we hung around too long Ed might be suspicious of your motives for returning home?'

'Yes.' She grinned, feeling in perfect harmony with him. 'We can pick up a hamburger in Castle Rock if you'd like.'

'I'd like.'

Tracy leaned back in her seat and stretched. Overhead, fast-moving clouds played peek-a-boo with the moon and stars. A steady stream of lights coming north was met by the continuous flow of traffic headed south. She took advantage of the dark to study Neil behind the wheel. His camel-hair jacket failed to hide his sartorial shortcomings. Even in the dark she could see the food stain on his shirt collar, and his expensive tie, which he'd tossed in the back, would be a challenge to any cleaner. Two tufts of hair stuck up like horns on his head, recalling to mind chubby little fists hanging on for dear life as he'd played pony, galloping sedately around the playroom floor.

Night fell long before they finally returned to Palmer Lake. Tracy had turned on the outside lights before they left and the yard was flooded with light. Wind bells hanging from the eaves pealed clamorously in the rising wind.

'Must be a chinook blowing in,' she said, unlocking the front door.

'What's a chinook?' A sudden gust whipped the bells into a wild frenzy, while nearby a small tree bowed to the ground, a gesture of obeisance before this Titan of the elements.

'It's a warm, downslope wind that brings a blast of warmer air with it.' She gestured about her. 'This snow will all be gone by morning. Feel how much warmer it is since this morning.'

Neil flinched as a gust rattled the very foundations of the house. 'Are we going to blow away?'

Half-way up the staircase, Tracy turned around. 'This is nothing. When the water in the toilet-bowl starts making tidal waves, then we can get concerned. Chinooks are a fact of life along the Front

Range. North of here, near Boulder, is supposed to be the third windiest spot in the world.'

'Statistics like that I don't need,' Neil grumbled.

Tracy laughed. 'Living in New York must make a person soft.'

'How can you say that? I risk my life every day on the subway or in taxis.'

'Big, brave Neil,' she mocked. 'While I'd love to stay and hear all about your daring exploits, I'm bushed. See you in the morning.' The howling of the wind drowned out Neil's reply.

The closing of her bedroom door was a signal for the thoughts and emotions that she'd been suppressing all day to come surging forth. Hands crossed beneath her head, Tracy stared blankly at the shadows gyrating madly across the bedroom ceiling. The rampaging wind outside paled in comparison to the storm which raged within her. This afternoon Neil Charles had breached the defences which she'd erected years ago around her heart. Disliking him had been easy when he'd constantly criticised and bullied her. Even their so-called truce had never hidden from her his implacable inner core. There was no denying his physical attraction, but that was sheer chemistry and would dissipate with his departure. She had been totally safe from Neil Charles.

Totally safe, that was, until four tiny, tear-filled blue eyes had turned him into a man that she would never have guessed even existed. After initially eyeing each other with misgiving, the twins and Neil had quickly formed a mutual admiration society. Neil had been patient, warm and loving, and his spontaneous delight in the operation of twenty tiny fingers and toes had disarmed Tracy. As for the twins, his unqualified adoration had quickly won their hearts. Tracy had even felt a twinge of jealousy as the girls cuddled and played with Neil, secure in their instinctive trust of him.

When Neil held her in his arms she, too, felt safe, but she knew such safety would vanish as quickly as the snow when the chinooks blew in. Not to be forgotten was that theirs was only a temporary truce. Tracy rolled on to her stomach and buried her face in her pillow. A sharp, ominous crack sounded outside. A branch from the old pine tree had been unable to withstand the destructive forces of the chinook.

She must have slept, because when she next looked at the ceiling the shadows had disappeared and the moon lit up her room. An odd feeling of disquiet stole over her and she lay motionless, her entire body listening. The night was still. Suddenly she relaxed. Of course. The wind had stopped. That must be what had awakened her. Punching her pillow into shape, she closed her eyes. A faint thud sounded from somewhere in the house. The loose shutter again.

Tracy sat up, swinging her legs over the side of the bed. The old oak floors froze her bare feet. Walking to the bedroom door she listened carefully. The noise was repeated. She'd have to go and secure the shutter. Without waking Neil.

The hall lights were out, but Tracy's eyes were used to the dark. As she started down the stairs the thudding sound repeated itself and a cold chill swirled around her feet. The window must have blown open. Near the bottom of the staircase she paused before negotiating the creaking stair tread. The silence was broken by the unmistakable sound of a soft footstep from the dining-room. Tracy froze in horror. The pitch-black hallway took on an ominous air, and she felt chillingly vulnerable standing there in her nightclothes, her ears straining to hear the slightest sound.

The house was still around her. Too still. Slowly she backed up the dark staircase. The sound of a footstep was not repeated, and she stopped. Had she really heard a noise, or was her imagination working overtime? She dared not rouse Neil for another non-existent burglar. The thudding sound repeated and she breathed a sigh of relief. It was only the shutter.

In the dining-room the window was partially open, the lace curtains stirring in the slight night breeze, sending goose-bumps up Tracy's spine. Even more chilling was the immense silhouette of a man tiptoeing towards the window. His furtive behaviour told Tracy instantly that, whoever was in the room with her, it wasn't Neil. Why hadn't she summoned him when she had had the chance? The man reached the window and ducked low, brushing the curtains aside. He was escaping.

Tracy was standing near the buffet, and without thinking she reached out and touched the hard, cold surface of a heavy brass candlestick. A few quick steps and she was across the room, the candlestick jabbing the intruder in the back. 'Hands up. I have a gun,' she said, her voice barely wobbling. 'It's a deer rifle that will splatter your innards all over the wall if you so much as breathe.' Poking the burglar's back for emphasis, she continued, 'And don't think I'm just some helpless woman.' Inspiration struck. 'Neil is standing right here beside me with a double-barrelled shotgun aimed right at your head. Neil, I'm going to call the sheriff now, so you blast this creep's brains all over my rug if he even thinks about turning his head.'

'I'd be more than happy to, but it's a little hard with my hands up in the air,' Neil said, his voice laced with amusement.

'Neil?' Tracy asked incredulously. 'Is that you?' She flipped on a switch. 'Why didn't you turn on the lights? You scared me half to death. I thought you were a burglar.'

Neil grinned at the brass candlestick gripped tightly in her hand. 'Splatter my innards?' he enquired with gentle sarcasm.

'It just popped out.' Tracy dropped on to a dining-room chair and stared wide-eyed at him. 'I could have shot you.'

He burst into laughter. 'With a candlestick?'

'If I'd really had a gun. You scared the heck out of me. What are you doing down here?'

'I thought I heard another loose shutter.' He frowned at her. 'Why did you open this window tonight?'

'I didn't.'

'I checked them all before I went to bed. It was locked.'

'I never replaced this window because of the leaded glass. The lock is ancient and the wind probably popped it open. It wouldn't be the first time.'

'What are you doing up?' Neil asked, leaning out of the window.

'I thought I heard a loose shutter, too. Then when I came in here and saw you tiptoeing across the room. . .' She shivered in the cold night air. 'Why were you sneaking around?'

'I wasn't sneaking,' he indignantly denied. 'I was trying not to wake you. That's strange,' he added a moment later. 'I could have sworn this was the loose shutter, but it's OK.'

'Maybe it was a basement window. I'm sure the noise came from this end of the house.' She swallowed a laugh. 'I can't believe how high you jumped when I poked you.'

He glared at her. 'So would you if someone stuck cold steel in your back.'

'Cold brass.'

'I defy you to tell the difference when it's stuck in your back.' His glare softened as he lowered his gaze.

Tracy had forgotten that she was clad only in a short ivory gown of silk and lace that provided expansive views of shoulders and thighs. Neil took the candlestick from her trembling fingers and set it down on the table. Her breathing quickened.

'You're hardly dressed for armed combat.' He toyed with a thin strap, his fingers burning a path across her skin.

Her racing pulse sent a flush of warm colour to her face and she quickly stepped back out of his reach. 'H-hadn't. . .' she cleared her throat, 'hadn't you better find the loose shutter?'

A crooked smile turned up one corner of Neil's mouth. 'I guess I had.' He turned away. 'Go on to bed.'

The draught from the open window had ravaged a bouquet of tulips on the table, and Tracy gathered up the scattered petals. She was throwing them in the kitchen rubbish bin when she heard the swearing from the basement. She ran down the stairs to be met by a blast of cold air. The old cellar doors, used years ago for coal deliveries and normally secured from the inside, lay opened flat on the ground.

'No wind did that,' Neil said flatly. 'There was an

intruder. He must have come in through the dining-room window and then, when he heard us, escaped through here.'

Tracy followed Neil up the steps to the outside. Shivering in the night air, she said, 'No footprints. The chinook has melted the snow.'

Far down the hill in the centre of town an engine started up and a car's lights flashed briefly. Tracy looked up at Neil. There was a grim smile on his face as he stared off into the distance. She shivered again. This time, not from the cold.

A large hand was curved intimately around her left breast. Tracy stiffened in shock, and then the memories of the previous night flooded over her. The intruder. The discovery that some boxes in the store-room had been broken into, their contents strewn over the concrete floor. The sheriff called out on what they all knew would be a fruitless errand. Most of the cartons that had been vandalised by the burglar were those she'd brought down from her parents' home and she had no idea what, if anything, was missing.

Tracy lay on her side on the very edge of the bed. Heavy breathing in the vicinity of her left ear told her that Neil was sleeping soundly behind her. His hand burned her skin. Tentatively, she shifted. Neil's hand tightened possessively. Her breast grew warm and turgid. She had to extricate herself before Neil awakened.

Why was he in her bed anyway? After the sheriff had left, a belated reaction to all that had happened had set in. What if she'd stuck the candlestick in some murderer's back instead of Neil's? What if the candlestick had been a gun and she'd shot Neil?

What if Neil hadn't awakened and the intruder had come upstairs into her bedroom? The stiffening had left her bones, she'd begun shaking uncontrollably, and hysteria had hovered near the surface. Neil had taken one look at her and made hot chocolate, after which he'd insisted on tucking her into bed. The panic in her voice when she'd refused to let him turn out her bedroom light had led to his offer to spend the night in her bedroom. An offer she'd immediately and gratefully accepted.

Which didn't quite explain the present situation. Neil had brought in a blanket from his room and, wrapping himself up in it, had lowered his long body into the old wicker armchair that sat next to her bed. The chair was empty now, its tenant obviously asleep beside her. She glanced down. Neil's body was putting out heat like a furnace and she must have pushed back her covers in her sleep. The buttons down the front of her gown had come loose and the edges gaped open. Neil's fingers were warm and her breast throbbed with desire. She fought the urge to press the swollen tip against his palm. If Neil awakened while they were joined in this intimate fashion. . .

Gingerly she placed her hand over Neil's and held her breath. When there was no reaction she gently, slowly, lifted his hand and carefully eased it over her shoulder. Her breath escaped in a slow sigh of relief.

'I'm glad you don't have any candlesticks in your bedroom.'

She jumped in surprise at the low, amused voice in her ear. 'Why?' The remark was so unexpected, it was impossible not to ask.

There were laughing undertones in his voice. 'I'd be afraid that you'd clobber me with one. I've been lying here awake for about five minutes, trying to figure out how to retrieve my hand without waking you.' The mattress shifted beneath his weight as he moved away from her. 'Talk about walking in one's sleep!'

Tracy clenched the covers firmly beneath her chin. If she moved any closer to the edge of the bed, she would fall out. Her robe hung in the closet across the room. As scantily dressed as she was, it might as well be on the moon. She glanced over her shoulder at Neil. He lay on his back on top of her covers, his blanket wrapped around him. The heat from his body warmed her through both sets of covers while his masculine, musky odour curled sensuously around her. 'I thought you were sleeping in the chair.'

'I was. And damned uncomfortable it was, too. You were lying here, snoring away, and——'

'I don't snore,' she interrupted.

'Snoring away,' he continued irrepressibly, 'and I had a crick in my neck, my legs kept going to sleep, and I noticed how you took up less than half the bed. The other half seemed like such a damned waste, lying there empty.'

It was quite clear that awakening in such a compromising position amused him. Tracy wished that she could laugh away her unsettled feelings so easily. Her voice was sharp with resentment. 'And such an opportunity, right?'

'An opportunity to straighten out before I turned into a pretzel,' Neil retorted. 'Believe it or not, I prefer my women awake and willing.'

CHAPTER EIGHT

'I'M happy to know that you have standards!' Tracy snapped.

'You don't sound so happy. Could it be that you're annoyed that I failed to ravage your body while you were sleeping?'

'That's ridiculous!'

'Is it?' He rolled over, his lips near her ear. 'I'll be happy to rectify the matter now that you're awake.'

'No, I——'

His mouth covered hers, cutting off any denial she might have made. At the first taste of his kiss she was powerless to resist, and willingly parted her lips to his questing tongue. Neil slid one leg possessively over her, pressing her intimately into the mattress. His blanket had slipped down to his waist and Tracy gloried in the feel of the warm, silken skin of his back beneath her hands, his muscles quivering to life at her touch. The scent of sandalwood filled her nostrils and her pulse quickened at the sound of his heavy breathing. Abandoning her mouth, he tipped back her head, exposing the throbbing pulse at the base of her neck to his hungry lips. The easy victory served only to whet his appetite, and the flimsy barrier of her blanket was quickly swept aside. Tracy felt a warm flush colour her skin at the low, guttural sound that came from Neil as her breasts were exposed to his gaze. His mouth followed his gaze and Tracy clung to his shoulders as hot waves of feeling, each more intense than the last, assaulted her body until she was trembling and weak in his embrace. When Neil lifted his head, she gasped for air, each breath overwhelming her with his heady, masculine scent. He rolled away and she shivered at the sudden loss of warmth.

'It's getting late. I need to call Jake about last night. I think it's time to force our murderer out in the open.' His voice was harsh as he rose from the bed.

'Why?' Tracy whispered, bewildered by his withdrawal.

'So I can get the hell out of here,' he said savagely.

'Oh.' That wasn't the question she'd wanted answered.

Neil whirled. 'Damn it, Tracy! Don't you know what almost happened here this morning? A few more minutes and I wouldn't have been able to stop.'

She sat up, the blanket clenched to her chest. 'I would have stopped you.'

Neil gave her a disparaging look. 'Face facts, Tracy. You would have let me make love to you, and what's more, you'd have enjoyed every minute of it.'

'That's not true.'

Neil grabbed her bare shoulders and yanked her to her knees. Tracy desperately clutched at the slipping blanket. His mouth came down hard on hers. Hanging on to the blanket with one hand, with the other she pushed against his bare chest. The curly mat of hair tantalised her palm. She knelt on the bed, unable to break away, her will and her body controlled by forces beyond her. She brought both hands up to toy with the silken strands of Neil's hair. For a moment the forgotten blanket hung on the swollen tips of Tracy's breasts, then it slithered with agonising slowness down her sensitised skin.

Maintaining his iron grip of her shoulders, Neil

took one step backwards. 'Now let's hear you deny that you want me to make love to you.' His thumbs pressed painfully into her flesh as his darkened eyes cynically surveyed her half-naked body.

Tracy closed her eyes, blotting out the betraying evidence of her own body. 'I hate you,' she choked.

'Good. Remember that.' Abruptly he released her.

'Neil.' She forced his name past the painful lump in her throat. 'Why?' Her courage almost quailed under the force of a bleak hazel gaze, but she forced herself to go on. 'Why do you want me to hate you?'

'Every time I look at you I ache with wanting to see you lying in my bed, your hair spread out on my pillow, your body soft and welcoming beneath me.'

His low, impassioned voice sent a thrill of desire through Tracy's body. A thrill quickly dashed by the remote look on Neil's face. 'I—I don't understand.'

'Some things just aren't meant to be. You and I. . .' He hesitated. 'You're Jake's daughter. As for me, I'm trusted by Jake. He'd never forgive me if I hurt you. And I would. It's better this way.' He left her without a backward glance.

Tracy huddled deep in the covers, seeking in vain to warm her shivering, chilled body. The smouldering heat of Neil's body was nothing more than a memory. She squeezed her eyes tightly against hot, threatening tears of humiliation. Neil had left her arms because he knew there was more to love than kisses that inflamed every fibre of one's being. Knowing that he was right did nothing to appease the emptiness that dwelt deep within her. Neil couldn't make love to her because he could never love her. Just as her father had never loved her. Just as her stepfather had never loved her. Her body curled up in misery. Even her mother had probably never loved her.

Neil banged on her door. 'The bathroom's free. Breakfast in twenty minutes.' He was gone before she could tell him she wasn't hungry.

The bathroom was warm and steamy. On any other chilly spring morning, Tracy might have appreciated that fact. This morning she grumbled beneath her breath about inconsiderate males as she used her towel to furiously wipe the steam from the mirror. Not that she wanted to use the mirror. Especially when it showed tousled hair, a flushed face and quivering lips. A faint whiff of Neil's aftershave hung in the moist air, the musky aroma a seductive reminder of his body heavy on hers. Forcibly rejecting the sensual image, Tracy stepped into the old-fashioned tub and twitched the plastic curtains into place for her shower.

When she came downstairs Neil was on the phone, his back to her. The delectable aroma of coffee and frying bacon hung in the air. Orange juice was beside her plate. Taking the glass, she wandered over to the kitchen window just in time to see the male bluebird fly from the birdhouse roof to a nearby low-hanging pine branch. From his new perch he surveyed the ground before making a sudden flight to the tulip bed. An insect grasped firmly in his beak, he flew back to the birdhouse where he clung to the front, his head disappearing into the opening. A love offering for his mate. She must have laid her eggs. Even while incubating the female would gather her own food, but an occasional urge to show his devotion would prompt the male to share a titbit with her. Sipping her juice, Tracy envied their uncomplicated life.

'I just finished talking to Jake.' Neil had returned.

She sat down. 'And?'

He set her coffee in front of her. 'I wanted him to know about the intruder. He'll get back to me.'

Tracy was proud of her outward serenity as she turned a mocking look on Neil. 'And what did *Daddy*,' her voice caustically underlined the last word, 'say when you told him you were in danger of being seduced by his little girl?'

Neil slammed down her plate. '"*Daddy*,"' he mimicked her intonation, 'didn't say anything, because I didn't tell him.'

'How honourable,' she cooed. 'You don't kiss and tell.'

'Keep it up, Tracy, and I'll strangle you myself.'

'There are worse things,' she said without thinking. A second later her horrified gaze met Neil's equally horrified one across the table.

He spoke first. 'I'm sorry, Tracy. I spoke without thinking. It was inexcusable for me to make such a tasteless remark after everything that has happened.'

'No, it was my fault.' She toyed with her scrambled eggs. 'I was trying to make you angry.' Her attempt at a smile was pathetic. 'The woman scorned and all that, I suppose.'

'Tracy, I. . .'

She shoved back her chair. 'No, don't.' Throwing her napkin on the table, she added, 'I'm not very hungry. I'll be in my workshop.' She practically ran from the kitchen.

The next few days were endless. Tracy spent every waking moment in her workshop, glad of an excuse to avoid Neil's company. She saw him only at mealtimes, when he treated her with polite formality. What he did to occupy his time she didn't ask; it was enough that he didn't seek her out. From the few remarks he uttered she knew that wheels were turning somewhere. What wheels and to what end she knew not. She only knew that the sooner the mystery was solved and the sooner Neil was out of her house, the happier she would be.

'Tomorrow should see the end of it,' he said abruptly at the dinner-table.

'Tomorrow?' Her stomach took an unpleasant dip.

'A trap has been set. Now we wait to see who shows up.'

Suddenly Tracy didn't want to know. A friend of Stan's. Someone he'd worked with, who'd eaten at their home. Someone he'd trusted and liked. Someone she knew. Her appetite faded and she laid down her fork. 'How. . .?'

Neil shook his head. 'That's not important.' A long silence hung over the table as Neil finished his dinner. Clearing the dishes, he said brusquely, 'I have to go up to Denver tomorrow afternoon, and I'll need to borrow your car.'

Tracy slid her dirty plate into the dishwater. 'Do you want me to come?'

'No.' He hesitated. 'You'll be safe here.'

The dishes were finished with a minimum of speech. Tracy wrung out the dishcloth and carefully draped it over the sink. 'I think I'll go back down to my workshop.'

Neil caught her arm as she turned away. 'About tomorrow. . .I just want to say. . .' He studied her face as if he were memorising every pore. 'I'm sorry.'

Shock momentarily paralysed Tracy. 'Is this goodbye?'

Neil shook his head. 'You'll understand tomorrow.'

The angry shrieks of the male bluebird wakened Tracy the next morning. Rushing to the window, she saw the bird darting frenziedly at the grass. Obviously he was trying to drive away an intruder, but Tracy could see no sign of one. Where was his mate? Haphazardly throwing on the first clothing that came to hand, she dashed down the hall.

Neil appeared at his bedroom door. 'What's going on?'

'I don't know. A squirrel or something at the bluebird house. The male is going crazy.' By the time she rounded the corner of the house, the backyard was silent. Ominously silent. The male bluebird was nowhere to be seen. Running to the garage, Tracy grabbed the metal step-ladder and, lugging it awkwardly under her arm, headed back to the birdhouse. Neil took it from her without a word.

Tracy lifted up the roof of the birdhouse with shaking hands. One look inside told the entire story of the tragedy. The undisturbed nest held no eggs and only a few bluish-grey feathers. The female had fought for her eggs. A losing battle.

'What happened?' Neil asked, looking at the empty nest.

'It must have been a snake. Any other predator would have destroyed the nest.

'How in the world could a snake get up this pole?'

'Snakes can climb. This one must have come while the male was away, so that he didn't have a chance to warn his mate to escape. If she had, they could have started a second family.'

Neil walked around the yard, his eyes cast downwards. 'I don't see any sign of a snake.'

'It's long gone by now. Chased away by the male.

No doubt down a hole or under a rock to allow its meal to digest.'

'We'd better check the other houses,' Neil said.

Tracy trailed disconsolately behind him. Even the sight of eight chickadee eggs and six nuthatch eggs intact in their nests failed to cheer her up. The two females, startled from their brooding chores by the raising of the roofs, sat on adjacent tree limbs protesting vociferously this human invasion of their privacy. 'Quit complaining. You're alive,' Tracy said.

'Come inside,' Neil urged. 'The dew is soaking your slippers. Let me fix you some breakfast.'

'I'm not hungry.'

'Starving won't bring back the bluebirds.'

'I know. Nothing will.' The tears gathered in the corners of Tracy's eyes. 'I feel so empty. Like—like. . .' Sadly she wiped the moisture from her eyes. 'It's an omen. There's not going to be any spring this year. At least, not for me.'

Tracy had not managed to shake off the sense of impending disaster by the time Neil left for Denver. Standing on her front porch, she watched her car disappear down the hill. Behind her the fiery sun dropped slowly down to greet the rising hills. The scent of pine hung in the afternoon air. A solitary dandelion, its bright yellow face mocking the spring-green lawn, grew impudently beside the driveway. The male chickadee, loudly declaring his name, sat atop his house, while in a nearby tree the male nuthatch noisily repeated his distinctive beep. An odd clicking sound from the juniper bushes betrayed a pair of juncoes. The area around the bluebird house was quiet. Far below, the lonely whistle of a train sounded. Tracy turned back towards her house. She had work to do.

Several hours later she put down the small brush that she was using to stain some wainscoting, unable to banish the uneasy feeling that gripped her. Upstairs in the kitchen, she stood silent, listening. Like any old house, hers was not a quiet one, but in the past the noises has been friendly like the greetings of old friends. Today the noises had been hostile, the house inimical to her presence. Outside, an owl hooted, raising the hair on the back of her neck. The doorbell pealed.

The shadow of a man was visible through the glass in the front door. Neil hadn't told her not to answer the door, but an odd reluctance to do so held her immobile in the kitchen doorway. The doorbell pealed again. Maybe it was one of her neighbours. The strident ring was urgent and demanding. Obviously the only way to get rid of her caller was to answer the door.

It was Blake. She stepped aside to allow him to enter. 'What brings you here?' she asked, her voice gay with relief.

'You.' He closed the front door firmly. 'We've played games long enough, Tracy. Where is it?'

'Where is what?'

'He told me that he had the proof, that he'd given it to someone. Who better than his own daughter?'

'Who had proof? Proof of what?' There was an odd, suppressed air of excitement about Blake that puzzled her.

'Very good, Tracy. If I didn't know better, I'd think you really didn't know.'

'I don't know what you're talking about.' She tried to ignore the terrible suspicion that clamoured to be heard.

Blake hunched his shoulders impatiently. 'The

proof,' he repeated in a harsh voice. 'The papers, the figures, the evidence, whatever he had. I told him I'd spare Maureen if he'd tell me. Unfortunately he got away from me and discovered her body. I had to kill him then. He went crazy. He would have killed me.' The note of disbelief in his voice added to the horrible unreality of the situation.

'You killed Stan and my mother?' This was a nightmare. It couldn't be happening. She swallowed hard, her nerves screaming at her to run. Blake stood between her and the door.

'I had to. He found out.' A flash of anger ignited his face. 'All that time finding a company with no sons to inherit, no old-timers waiting to step into the presidency. I was supposed to take over when Stan retired. Damn him for planning to sell the business right out from under me!' Blake kept pace with her as she stepped backwards.

'You knew that he planned to sell?' Her mind refused to accept what was happening.

'Of course I did. He told me first. In case I wanted to make other arrangements. So generous,' Blake said with a contemptuous curl of his lip. 'Only before he could sell there would have to be an outside audit. I couldn't have that.'

'It was you! You embezzled the money. Why?' There must be some mistake. This was Blake. Not a murderer.

'Don't be naïve. How could I live on what Stan paid me?'

'He paid you well.' Her heel slammed into the bottom stair, and she would have fallen if she hadn't grabbed the newel.

'So speaks the millionaire's daughter,' he sneered.

'No more talk. I want those papers. Give them to me.'

'I don't have them.' She'd managed to edge around the staircase. The kitchen door was only about five feet away.

Blake smiled. A cold, cruel smile. He pulled a bedraggled red tie from his pocket.

'That's Neil's tie,' she said in astonishment.

'I know.' He wrapped it first around one fist, then the other, a length of tie between his two hands. 'I took it from the back seat of your car the night I broke into the basement.'

'That was you?' What she was thinking was impossible. Still, held that way, the tie looked. . .'What are. . .are. . .you . . .why. . .Neil's tie?' she stuttered. The sound of fear in her voice disgusted her. She couldn't drag her eyes from his hands.

'You should have stayed in Denver that night, like you told me. Then we could have prevented this little unpleasantness. I would have found the proof. I couldn't get in the Denver house, but it was in those boxes with your name on it, wasn't it?'

Fighting the compulsion to stare at the tie jerking in Blake's hands, she forced her chin up. 'No. There was nothing there.' The crazy light that flared in Blake's eyes sent a shaft of terror straight to her brain. He was insane. The realisation that she was about to die hit her with such horrible, terrifying force that she was unable to prevent herself from abandoning her cautious movements, and she took two quick steps backwards. The telephone-table brought her up short. The telephone! Why hadn't she thought of it earlier? Willing Blake not to notice, she slowly reached behind her back. Her face must have betrayed her.

'Keep away from the phone.' His voice lashed sharply out.

Tracy dropped her hand. 'Neil will be back soon.'

'Your boyfriend is sitting in a Denver bar waiting for me. My comments about Stan going crazy have him all excited, thinking he can break Stan's will so that the plant will go to you. He's stupid enough to think I'll help him.' His grin was evil. 'Too bad you had a lover's quarrel and he killed you.'

'You won't get away with this. Neil will tell them. . .'

'What?' Blake laughed. 'My calendar says our meeting is tomorrow, and my landlady will swear she heard me at home tonight. It's wonderful how electronics can make an empty apartment appear to be occupied. As for Neil——' He shrugged. 'A man so greedy. The police won't find it difficult to believe that he strangled you and then burned down your house to cover his crime.'

'Burn down my house?' Her brain was refusing to take in the things he was saying in his horrible, gloating voice.

'How else can I make sure to get all the evidence?' He started towards her, the red tie a slash of blood.

'If you burn down the house, how will anyone know that I've been murdered?' she asked hastily. Time. She needed more time.

'Arson is so difficult to hide these days. I don't doubt that they can sift enough clues from the ashes to figure out the entire crime. In fact,' he paused, malevolence darkening his eyes, 'I'm counting on it. There's something about Neil Charles that I don't like.'

'The feeling is mutual.'

The voice came from behind Tracy, from upstairs. Hard, full of anger. The most beautiful sound in the world. Neil.

A look of rage crossed Blake's face; his teeth bared in a furious grimace. 'You're supposed to be in Denver!'

'This seemed like a better place to meet you.' Neil paused before adding in a deliberate taunt, 'You shouldn't have made the mistake of thinking that I'm as stupid as you are.' His firm footsteps descended the staircase.

The touch of Neil's hand on her shoulder sent such a shudder of relief through Tracy that she almost collapsed. 'I thought you were gone,' she breathed. His hand tightened reassuringly.

'You made one mistake right after the other from the very beginning. Not very smart, even for a criminal,' Neil said conversationally. 'You might have got away with everything if you'd left Tracy alone. She doesn't know anything.' Casually, Neil pushed Tracy's leaden body behind him.

Blake's face twisted in a horrible grimace of hate. '*You*,' he said, his voice filled with loathing. 'If you hadn't been staying with Tracy this would have been over long ago.' He hurtled towards Neil, his hands coming up so quickly that all Tracy saw was a blur of red.

Quick as Blake was, Neil was quicker. In the blink of an eye, Blake was lying stretched out on the wooden floor. Neil rubbed his fist. 'I guess I finally pushed him too far.'

'That sort can't bear to think someone outsmarted them.' A solidly built older man came out of Tracy's living-room.

The hall filled with men. Local law enforcement. She'd finally placed the older man; he was from Denver. There were other Denver detectives. Tracy watched numbly as they roughly hustled Blake to his feet and hauled him out of the front door.

'You OK?' Neil asked.

'Y-yes.' If one discounted shaking knees and a heart that pounded so fast that the blood was humming in her ears. 'I can't believe it. Blake? Blake was the one who embezzled, and he murdered Mother and Stan when Stan discovered it?'

Neil nodded wearily. 'Yes.' He looked over her shoulder. 'Here's someone who can explain it better than I can.'

There was an odd note in Neil's voice. Tracy swiftly turned around. A tall, grey-haired man was walking out of her kitchen. A faint air of concern clung to him; his steel-blue eyes asked her a question. Slowly Tracy backed away from him, shaking her head in denial. She couldn't breathe. The light from the chandelier began to bounce around the hallway, the terrifying balls of light assaulting her. Walls closed in on her and then started whirling around. Faster. Faster.

The man frowned at her. 'Tracy?'

Everything went mercifully black.

When Tracy opened her eyes, she was lying on the sofa in her front parlour. A slender woman with stylish short brown hair was standing beside her. Tracy had never seen her before.

The woman saw Tracy looking at her. 'How do you feel?'

'OK.' She didn't want to talk. If she started talking she might ask questions. Questions to which she didn't want the answers. She didn't care where Neil was. She didn't want to know if that had been her father in the hall. She wasn't interested in who this woman was—this woman who looked so much like Neil. Cautiously she sat up. The room remained in place.

The woman was carefully appraising her. 'You scared us.'

'Did I?' asked Tracy, with total lack of interest.

A wary looked flickered across the woman's face. 'I don't blame you for being angry. Jake had no business using you as a decoy without your permission. Even if Neil did spend the day smuggling law officers into the house. Jake and Neil both insisted that you'd be safer if you didn't know.'

That explained all the sounds she'd heard.

'Tracy's every thought is broadcast by her face. She couldn't have deceived Blake for a second.'

Tracy jerked her head around to see Neil lounging in the doorway, a different Neil, a stranger. Tracy looked down, focusing on the tightly clenched fists in her lap. The soft voices of Neil and the woman flowed over her. Other voices, strange male voices, drifted in from the hall.

'She OK?' The deep, anxious voice brought her head sharply back up. He stood beside Neil. 'Tracy?'

She looked away.

The painful silence was broken by Jake Archer. 'I thought you might like an explanation for all of this,' he said curtly.

'Yes.' Her fists tightened their grip.

'It's difficult to pinpoint where Blake started going wrong. Maybe back when his father was fired, destroying the elder Campbell's self-esteem and turning him into a bitter man who deserted his family. Blake grew up thinking that "big business" owed him something. He wanted money and status. So he turned to stealing. He thought he was too smart to be caught. There were no troubling morality problems because he never viewed Warner's company as a group of people, but as an anonymous organisation.'

'But Stan was good to him,' Tracy blurted out. 'He must have known that embezzling from his company would hurt Stan.'

'Blake held Stan in the highest contempt. He had no patience with Stan's integrity, which he felt cost the company money. Blake is motivated by a desire to beat the other guy. The only thing he admired about Stan was his bank account and his social standing. By beating Stan, he seemed to think he would become magically endowed with both.' Jake shook his head. 'Revenge, greed, envy, a pathological desire to be at the top of the heap. Blake was a human bomb just waiting to explode.'

'And when Maureen thought she was ill, Stan decided to sell the company to spend more time with her. Detonating the bomb.'

Jake nodded in agreement with Neil's statement. 'He'd been embezzling right from the beginning to maintain the style of living he believed he was entitled to. He felt safe because he figured on taking over the company when Stan retired, but then Stan told him about the potential sale and Blake panicked. Stan grew suspicious and started a small investigation on his own. Blake found out and he murdered Stan and Maureen.'

'But why?' Tracy burst out. 'Embezzlement would only have meant a few years in jail, at the most. But murder!'

'Being found guilty would have sentenced Blake to a lifetime of disgrace, his dreams of wealth and success forever buried. The irony is that Stan's concern for Blake ultimately led to the murders. If he hadn't told Blake his plans. . .' Jake shrugged. 'I'm not a psychiatrist, but I can't help but wonder if subconsciously Blake didn't see Stan as a substitute father, and when he discovered that Stan was deserting him also, he simply went berserk.'

'There's no point in dwelling on that,' the woman said briskly. 'It's over now, and Tracy is safe.'

Over. The word stabbed painfully at Tracy. Her glance flew to Neil. He'd moved and was looking out of the window into the darkness. She forced herself to look at Jake. 'How long before I get the papers on the house?'

Disappointment flashed across her father's face. 'My office is working on transferring the entire estate right now.'

'Jake?' The woman spoke up. 'Why don't you ask Tracy now?'

'Uh—sure—um. Tracy, I—uh. . .' Nervously he ran his finger along the inside of his collar. 'That is, Susan and I wondered if you, maybe, would come stay with us for a while?'

'Susan?'

Jake walked over to the woman and put his arm around her. 'I guess you two haven't really met. Susan is my wife.'

'And my mother,' Neil said heavily.

His words hung in the silent room. Tracy closed her eyes against the stabbing pain. She'd known from the moment she'd seen the woman's hazel eyes. Neil's eyes. From the beginning she'd realised there could be only one reason why Neil's mother would be here. Because she was Jake's wife. Neil was Jake's stepson. The son he preferred over his own daughter. 'You might have told me,' she said to Neil.

He took a step towards her. 'Tracy, I can explain.'

She put up her hand to ward him off. 'I can't imagine how. I should be thankful that you at least had the decency to change your mind about seducing me.'

'What does that mean?' Jake grabbed Neil's arm.

'Yes, tell your daddy dearest what good and intimate friends we've become,' Tracy crooned maliciously.

Neil shook off Jake's grip. 'It's not what you think?'

'Are you denying that you spent a night in my bed?' Tracy demanded.

'Is this true? My daughter? Why, you filthy. . .' Jake lunged towards Neil, his face mottled with rage.

'Stop it!' Susan moved swiftly to stand between them.

'Get out of the way!' Jake roared. 'I'm going to kill him.'

'Let the old guy give me his best punch,' Neil said wearily. 'He can't hurt me, and I promise you I won't touch him.'

'Why, you snot-nosed little kid, I'll wipe up the floor with you.' Jake clenched his fists and shadow-punched at the air.

Tracy had had enough. 'I'm going to my room,' she said, her icy voice cutting through the air like a knife. 'I would appreciate it if you would lock the front door behind you when you leave.' She refused to look at any of them.

Once out of the room, she dropped all pretence of control and raced up the stairs. The dead silence she left behind her erupted into a sharp argument.

Tracy locked her bedroom door and threw herself on the bed. No wonder Neil hadn't wanted to talk about Jake's stepson.

Downstairs the loud noises ceased. In the ensuing silence Tracy heard Neil's pounding footsteps taking the stairs three at a time. He rattled sharply on the door. When there was no response, he rattled the handle vigorously.

'Go away!' Tracy spat. 'You've had your fun.' She pressed a pillow over her ears.

'Damn it, Tracy.' An explosive crash echoed throughout the house and then Neil stood in the open doorway, the wood-panelled door hanging drunkenly from its hinges. 'I said I wanted to talk to you.' He stalked into the room, his jaw tight with anger.

Tracy jumped to her feet and flung her pillow at him. Standing between her and the door, he batted it to the floor. There was no escape. 'All right, talk,' she said sullenly. She didn't have to listen.

The anger drained from his face and he shifted his gaze to somewhere behind her. 'I should have told you,' he said. 'At first it didn't occur to me, and then later, when I realised that it mattered to you, I couldn't tell you precisely because it did matter. You'd never have let me stay, and protecting you was the most important thing.'

'Those pathetic stories about how hard you worked during college,' she sneered. 'Lies. Jake put you through school. How you must have resented having to share the largesse with Jake's daughter.'

He rejected her accusations. 'My mother gave a party for me when I graduated from law school, and she invited Jake. They'd never met before. They were married six months later.'

In her anger and hurt, his words meant nothing to her. 'How diabolically clever you were!' she marvelled. 'You didn't want me to patch things up with my father. All that talk about how much you worship him. You knew that I resented it and hoped that I'd never forgive him. But just in case, oh, that was very clever of you. . .you couldn't risk Jake's leaving me everything, but if I were in love with you. . .how far were you prepared to go? Marry me? I suppose you would have been a widower at an early age. Blake Campbell could have learned from you,' she charged.

'That's unfair.' He walked over to the window and stood looking out into the night, his hands jammed into his pockets.

'You're a fine one to talk about fair. You've been lying and deceiving me the whole time.'

'I've never lied to you.'

'You lied by omission. Don't deny it. When I asked you about Jake's stepson——'

'Jake's stepson is a mythical person who exists only in your mind. Damn it, Tracy, I was twenty-five years old when my mother married him, and I'm thirty-one now. Jake has never tried to replace my father. We're friends. Or *were*.' He stressed the last word. 'He just fired me because I refused to make an honest woman of you.' The flat statement came over his shoulder without warning.

Tracy clung to the headboard of her bed, the metal cold and lifeless against her skin. 'I hope you're not expecting sympathy from me,' she said, fighting to keep her voice emotionless.

Neil turned at her words. 'I wouldn't dare, would I? After all the times I withheld it from you.'

For a moment the deeply suppressed pain managed to surface, but Tracy ruthlessly shoved it back under lock and key. 'It's been a long day. I'd appreciate it if you'd leave.'

Neil's eyes narrowed to dark slits. 'Kicking me out?'

'Your job is done. I see no reason for you to hang around.'

'I see.' He moved towards her, his eyes locked with hers, only stopping when he was directly in front of her. 'Don't you?'

'No.'

Neil lifted his hands to her shoulders and lightly massaged her tense muscles. His penetrating stare was too much for her and she dropped her eyes. He gave a deep grunt of satisfaction and, bending his head, pressed his lips against her mouth. She neither fought him nor responded, but simply stood there, enduring his kiss. He lifted his head. 'It appears that this is goodbye.'

'Yes.' Every muscle in her body quivered at his nearness.

He walked away from her, turning when he reached the door. 'Jake is still downstairs. Do you want to see him?'

Her grip tightened on the bed. 'Does he want to see me?'

'I don't know. I can ask him.'

'No.' The back of her throat filled with tears. 'It's too late. Fifteen years too late.'

Neil studied her face. 'Pride is a lonely friend.'

'I have other friends.'

He hesitated, prepared to argue, but the look on her face must have stopped him. 'All right.'

His retreating footsteps drove splinters into her heart. Every nerve in her body, every muscle, cried out to him not to go away, not to leave her. He didn't hear.

Downstairs the doorbell rang and she could hear his voice talking to someone. Other voices joined in and then she quit listening, surrendering at last to the excruciating pain she was no longer capable of fighting.

She was sitting on the edge of her bed, stiffly rocking back and forth, a pillow clutched against her stomach, when Jess walked into her room. 'Has he left?' Tracy asked.

'Who? Neil or your dad? They've both left.'

The look of commiseration on Jess's face was more than Tracy could bear. She burst into tears.

CHAPTER NINE

JESS dropped her parcels on to the rusty pink banquette in the Rattlesnake Club's downstairs grill and slid in beside them with a hugh sigh of relief. 'Wasn't I right? Wasn't getting out of the house today just what you needed?' she demanded.

'It may have been what I needed, but I'm not sure if your cheque-book needed it,' Tracy said drily, with a significant look at Jess's purchases. Underneath the table she kicked off her shoes and unobtrusively wiggled her tired feet. Only a few of the tables were occupied, with most of the patrons out on the enclosed patio taking advantage of the late-afternoon views seen through enormous Palladian-styled windows. After dragging her up and down the length of the 16th Street mall all morning, Jess had charged over to Tivoli Denver, the recently built shopping centre, for the afternoon. Struggling along in her wake, Tracy had finally begun to snap out of the dazed stupor that had engulfed her since that fateful night. A week had passed since Blake had come to kill her. A week since Neil had walked out of her house. A week since Jess had come down to Palmer Lake and gathered up the shaking, hysterical hull that was Tracy and taken her back to the Baldwins' home in Denver.

The time had come to forget what had happened and gather the remnants of her life about her again. She sipped the wine that Jess had ordered. 'I think I'll go back home tomorrow.'

'There's no rush,' Jess said quickly. 'You've been through quite an ordeal. Every time I think about how they set the trap with you as the bait, I get furious all over again.'

Tracy shrugged. 'With all those policemen, I was never in any danger.'

'I knew they suspected someone, but I never dreamed it was Blake,' she said, her voice tinged with horror. 'How he could. . .' Catching the look on Tracy's face, she briskly changed the subject. 'The point is, Ed and I are enjoying your company and don't want you to rush back home.'

'Is that so? Then how come very night after dinner Ed is so visibly happy when I announce it's my bedtime.'

Lovely colour washed over Jess's cheekbones. 'It's not that Ed isn't happy to have you,' she started to explain.

'You don't need to draw me any pictures,' Tracy said. 'I'm glad that you and Ed have worked things out.'

Jess reached across the table and squeezed Tracy's hand. 'It doesn't seem fair that I should be so happy right now.'

'Why? Because of what happened?'

'I don't like to see you so unhappy. Ed told me to mind my own business, but. . .' Jess traced the edges of the pink and peach squares in the black table-top with her fingernail.

'But what?' A feeling of foreboding crept over Tracy.

'Well,' Jess said evasively, 'when I was miserable, you helped me. . .so. . .' She attempted a half-hearted smile.

'What have you done?' Tracy clenched her fists in

her lap beneath the table-top. The answer came immediately.

'I hope I haven't kept you waiting,' Neil said, his glance flickering over Tracy to settle on Jess. 'Quite an interesting place here.'

'It's the old Tivoli Brewery,' Jess quickly explained, darting nervous glances at Tracy. 'The building was declared a historic landmark in 1973 and then developed into a shopping centre. Some of the centre is new construction, but we're in the original part. You probably walked past the old boiler-room, and these copper things over our heads are the original brewing kettles. The kettles are two storeys high and could brew three hundred thousand barrels of beer a year.' The nervous, high-pitched spate of words fell into an unrelenting void.

Neil turned to Tracy. 'Jake is leaving tomorrow. No,' he added quickly at her sudden gesture of denial. 'I'm not going to ask you to see him. He doesn't even know that I'm here. And don't blame Jess for this. I asked her to make the arrangements. She had no choice.'

'She could have said no.' Tracy finally found her voice.

The waiter set a glass in front of Neil and he took a long drink. 'She agrees with me that you ought to know the truth about what happened all those years ago.'

'I'm not interested,' Tracy said stiffly. Neil couldn't possibly have anything to say that was of interest to her. The silence was deafening. Tracy dropped her gaze before the look of disappointment in Jess's eyes. It wasn't Jess's business, Tracy thought defensively, bracing herself for the arguments and guilt-laden charges that Neil would make.

He sighed heavily. 'All right.'

The floor was carpeted, but the sound of the chair sliding away from the table was the knelling of doom in Tracy's head. 'No,' she said abruptly, her glance bouncing off Neil's face. 'I'll listen.'

'Without prejudice?' he asked evenly.

'I can't promise anything, but I'll try.'

'Fair enough.' Neil pulled his chair back to the table.

Jess stood up. 'I just remembered. I have to buy a birthday present for Ed's mom. I'll be back.' She was gone before Tracy could protest.

Neil gave Tracy a swift, guarded look. 'Some of this I knew. The rest I found out from my mother this week. Jake has told Mother very little about his marriage to your mother, but it must have been a mistake from the beginning. They lived with her parents and Jake hated it. He felt like an object of their charity, but at the same time he saw the force of their argument that Maureen was accustomed to better than he could afford. Maybe if he'd been older and more mature he could have handled it, but their money and background must have made him feel insecure. His answer to that was to work unspeakably hard to make his own fortune. Of course, that meant lots of time away from home and family. Maureen didn't understand what drove him, and their lack of communication drove a wedge of enormous proportions between them. Finally, you were the only reason he went home at all.'

'I wasn't much of a reason either, was I?' Tracy asked bitterly. 'He had no trouble leaving me.'

'She kicked him out,' Neil said. 'I'm not saying the failure of the marriage was your mother's fault. Jake had too much pride. If she couldn't understand; he wasn't about to explain. There were other women. And he was foolish. He threw the other women in her face. She hired a private detective and there was evidence—receipts, pictures. Naturally she got everything she wanted.' He took another drink.

Tracy traced around the rim of her glass with her finger. In the silence that settled over their table she could hear the murmur of voices from the other inhabitants of the room.

'All he asked for in exchange was partial custody of you. And, up to the last minute, she led him to believe that he would get it. Then she came in with her big guns. A maid who was willing to testify that he had an uncontrollable temper. A psychiatrist who made much of your being turned into a "wishbone child", pulled in opposite directions by parents who hated each other. There was more. Lots more. Fighting it all would have meant a vicious courtroom custody case. Jake realised that no matter who won custody, you were going to be the big loser. He loved you too much to subject you to that.' He studied her across the table. 'Jake sent you letters and presents by the carload for the first few years. Then, when you were about twelve or thirteen, he received a typewritten letter from you saying that you wished he'd stop pestering you, that Stan had become your father.'

'I never received anything from him, and I never sent him any such letter. No one would even tell me his address.'

'Jake kept the letter. He showed it to my mother once after their marriage when she was asking about you. She said the signature was definitely juvenile.' He paused before adding in a non-committal voice, 'It was probably traced.'

'Is that why you hated me? Because of the letter?'

'No. I didn't know about that. It was the other letters. Jake would get one and go into such a deep depression that the entire office grew to hate the sight of a Colorado postmark.'

Tracy stiffened. 'You mean she sent other letters alleged to be from me?' Neil had carefully avoided placing blame, but only her mother would have done such a thing.

'No. Stan wrote.'

'Stan?' Tracy echoed in astonishment.

'Stan felt that Jake had been dealt with unfairly in the matter of his daughter. At the same time, Stan would never do anything to upset or hurt your mother. He approached Jake and told him that if Jake would cease trying to contact you and upsetting Maureen, he would send him regular letters—progress reports, really—on you. Jake debated, but finally decided that any contact was better than none at all.' Neil studied the copper kettle overhead. 'The letters were very impersonal. Jake kept them in a file. He showed them to me before I flew out here. Your grades, what activities you were in. Your horse, your ballet lessons. Going to camp every summer. Your début. College comings and goings. They made you sound. . .' He stopped abruptly.

'I know. Like a rich, spoiled brat.' She bit her lower lip. 'I wondered why Stan wrote to Jake about the problems at the plant. I suppose writing those other letters gave him the idea.'

'Probably.' Neil's gaze settled on her face. 'I told Jake that you didn't write the letter, didn't know about the allowance.' His voice grew harsh. 'I told him what your mother had done.'

'It doesn't matter any more.' She blinked unshed

tears from her eyes and pretended to be absorbed in watching two women climb the turquoise staircase. 'She's dead.'

'It matters to the living. You and Jake.'

Tracy shook her head. 'You're wrong. It doesn't matter to him. If it did. . .' She sipped her drink. Jake Archer had made no attempt to contact her since the night of Blake's arrest.

'He's afraid.'

Her astonished gaze met Neil's challenging one. 'Afraid of what?'

'You. He admits that he rushed your mother into marriage, and he's always blamed himself for the divorce. And now he thinks he failed you, that he should have fought harder for custody. He knows you blame him. You demonstrated that the other night.' Neil reached across the table and covered her hand with his. 'He needs you.'

Tracy snatched back her hand. 'He has his wife. And you.'

Neil gave a weary sigh. 'Let's not start that again.' Reaching inside his sports jacket, he pulled out a card. 'Jake's phone number and address.' Grabbing her hand, he turned it over and laid the card across her palm. 'Give him a chance, Tracy. He's never stopped loving you.' He curled her fingers around the card and stood up. 'Here comes Jess.'

'Thank you for telling me all that,' she said formally. 'I'll think about what you said.' She watched Jess wend her way through the tables towards them.

'Tracy,' his voice was tense, 'my phone number and address are on the card, too. If you ever need me. . .'

Tracy's hand tightened convulsively around the card, crumpling it into a ball. A ball that burned her skin. She opened her fist. The crumpled wad fell into the empty ashtray.

Neil turned and walked from the restaurant. He hadn't said one word about the fact that he'd rather lose his job than marry her. Not that she cared.

Three weeks later Tracy was still trying to convince herself on that point. The Victorian doll's house sat in front of her on the workbench. She'd be glad when it was finished and gone. Too many memories. She traced the round stained-glass window in the staircase wall with an unsteady finger. She'd been making that window the day the police had called her to tell her the tragic news about Stan and her mother.

And the small front door. Every time she looked at it she could see Neil's hazel eyes peering through. The sight of the miniature marble fireplaces instantly conjured up a mental picture of Neil's hands caressing the white marble, caressing her. . . She squeezed her eyes tightly in a futile effort to blot out the memories.

If only she could go back to that day in Ed's office. A kinder fate would have prevented her from agreeing to Jake Archer's stipulation. How ironic that, now she no longer cared whether or not she stayed in the house in Palmer Lake, it belonged to her. The envelope lay on the workbench where she'd tossed it. Unopened. The house was nothing but a bunch of boards. Her boards.

She'd been a fool. And all because of a childish belief that her grandmother's house welcomed her. Because, in the end, it was the house that was betraying her. Everywhere she looked there were reminders of Neil. She had only to pass the empty guest bedroom to be overwhelmed by the image of Neil sleeping, bare to the waist. The staircase brought back memories of Neil in his outrageous briefs, while the sight of a candlestick set her heart pounding. She'd scoured the bathroom endlessly, but the scent of sandalwood soap refused to fade away. He even haunted the sanctuary of her room. Her bed, the wicker chair, the sound of the wind at night—they all brought back memories: the night she'd awakened him, the night she'd followed him to Estemere, the night he'd stayed with her to calm her fears, the morning he'd awakened beside her. . .the morning he'd rejected her. It all came back to that. Neil had rejected her. Twice.

It would be funny if it weren't so pathetic. Tracy Warner, who knew better than anyone the perils of loving, had fallen in love. It was no longer possible to deny it. She even knew the exact moment. Neil had been standing barefoot in Jess's tub, his clothes stained with baby food, and he'd looked over at her and smiled. Her stomach had done an immediate flip-flop. Even then she'd tried to deny the truth.

Because she'd been warned. Neil had told her from the beginning that he didn't like her. She hadn't liked him either. He'd been hard and ruthless. He still was. There had been no mercy in him for Blake. But living with him had shown her other qualities. His patience with the twins. Loyalty to Jake. Intelligence. He'd been kind when she'd been so afraid the night Blake had broken into the house. Concerned about Jess and Ed. Amusing. Secure enough in his masculinity to cook and clean.

A sharp thrill ran through her body. For a woman who disliked violence, she'd felt a certain primitive excitement when Neil had punched Blake. At the time she'd believed that the blow was as much for

Blake hurting her as in self-defence. Then had come Neil's refusal to marry her.

Once more, against all wisdom, she'd given away her heart. Only to have it thrown back in her face. She twisted her lips in a mocking caricature of a smile. So much for her precious avowals to never need anyone's love again.

The envelope drew her gaze. The return address was impersonal. A law firm. Cold and forbidding. Not from her father. She'd finally found the couarge to read the magazine article that Neil had given her. The story and trappings of Jake's accomplishments were not unexpected, nor was she surprised that his second marriage was judged a success. What had astounded her was the reporter's opinion that Jake Archer's estrangement from his daughter had left a void in his life that no amount of succes could fill.

Could it possibly be true? He'd sent Neil out to protect her. He'd come himself at the end. And she'd snubbed him. Because all these years she'd believed that he'd rejected her. The truth was that her father had loved her enough to put her happiness ahead of his. He'd loved her enough to give her up.

Tracy picked up the envelope and slit it open with a small knife. It was full of official-looking papers. And one small note ripped from a memo pad. 'I'm here if you need me.' He'd signed his initials. After fifteen years he was afraid to call himself her father.

The next move was up to her. She'd forgiven her mother. After three long weeks she'd finally come to grips with her mother's betrayal. Her mother had loved her. And, loving her daughter, Maureen had feared losing her, so she'd lied. Tracy couldn't change the past, but she could shape her own future.

By the time she'd worked her way through a legion

of secretaries, Tracy's nerve had badly slipped. She still hadn't decided what she would say when Jake finally came on the phone.

'Tracy, is that really you?'

At the betraying wobble of uncertainty in his voice all of Tracy's fears and doubts fled. 'Daddy. . .' The painful lump in her throat prevented further speech.

'Honey, I'm so glad you called. I've missed you so much.'

Suddenly it was all right. 'I've missed you, too.'

Jake cleared his throat. 'If you only knew how often I've dreamed of this moment. I love you, honey.'

'I know. Neil told me.' She hesitated. 'You shouldn't have fired him. Nothing happened.'

'Don't worry, he's still here. I'm always firing him. He's the only guy in the office with the guts to stand there and tell me to my face when I'm wrong. So I fire him, and then, when I cool down, I rehire him. I'm afraid your old man has quite a temper.'

Tracy laughed. The tinge of pride in his rueful voice hadn't escaped her. 'I know. Neil told me that, too.'

'I suppose he also told you about me going off half-cocked and telling him that he had to marry you?' Jake's voice was gruff with embarrassment. 'All the things I've ever said to the kid, and that's the first time I thought that he was going to haul off and slug me. He stuck his nose in my face and said that you were worth ten of me if I was accusing you of sleeping around. That it was an insult to both of you, and that if you slept with a man it would be because you loved him, and when you did it was none of my business.'

Tracy gripped the phone in astonishment. 'Neil said that?'

'Neil said a lot of things,' her father replied. 'Did I make a mistake sending him out there?'

'No—I mean, why do you ask? He kept me in one piece, didn't he?'

'You tell me.'

'I don't know what you mean,' Tracy evaded.

'They don't come much better than Neil.'

'I'm sure that he's an excellent lawyer. . .'

'His mom swears he picks up his socks, puts the cap on the toothpaste and cooks a decent meal.'

'I know. And he buys Girl Scout cookies.'

'What?'

'Never mind. How are the Mets doing?'

'Not bad. You still squirt more mustard on your shirt than on your hot dog?'

'I—I don't watch baseball much any more.'

The silence stretched uncomfortably long over the telephone wires. Then Jake sighed. 'I'm sorry, honey. I just wish I could make it up to you.' After a short pause, he added in a diffident voice, 'You could come out, and we'll take in some games and I'll buy you all the hot dogs and mustard you want.'

Tracy could hear the plea behind the teasing. 'I—I'd like that, but I have to finish this doll's house first.'

Her father accepted her answer, asking her interested and knowledgeable questions about her work. It was obvious that Neil had told him all about it. One topic led to another, and over an hour passed before Tracy replaced the receiver with trembling hands.

The conversation with her father had given her a great deal to think about. Fifteen years lost because each had believed lies about the other and both had been afraid to seek out the truth. Fear. It was a weakness, and yet such a powerful emotion. One that could drive people to desperate measures. Her mother, afraid of losing those she loved, driven to lying. Blake, afraid of being poor, driven to theft and murder.

If it hadn't been for her own weakness, Blake would have been apprehended much earlier. Because he'd been right all along—Stan had given her the proof. Unable to concentrate on her work one day, she'd picked up the birdhouse she'd made for her stepfather. Lost in her self-pitying thoughts, she'd barely been aware of opening the roof. Even now it seemed so unbelievable. If only she hadn't associated the birdhouse with unhappy memories and had let Neil put it up. Tracy doubted that she would ever know the circumstances that had prompted her stepfather to roll up the papers that were evidence of Blake's guilt and hide them in a useless niche in the birdhouse.

Talking for so long had left her throat dry. In the kitchen she stared out of the window, sipping water. The fledgling nuthatches had abandoned her yard for the woods, but several baby chickadees, looking like roly-poly miniature dusters, sat on a budding tree limb. A flash of blue caught Tracy's eye, and she watched in surprise as the male bluebird flew from the birdhouse.

Minutes later she climbed down a rickety metal ladder, torn between happiness and utter disbelief. Granted that she had practically lived in her workshop since returning from Denver. Granted that her thoughts had been involved in an inward struggle of mammoth proportions. Even so, how could she have missed the fact that the male bluebird had found another mate? Glancing up, she spotted the male sitting on a nearby branch watching her.

'Think you're pretty clever, don't you?' Laughter bubbled up within her. The first laughter in weeks. 'Four strong, healthy, hungry babies. You'd better get busy.' The female landed nearby, her beak filled with a large insect.

The babies were pink and scrawny with enormous yellow beaks. She could picture the laughter in Neil's eyes if he saw them. Neil. Her father's words came back to her. Neil had flouted Jake's order to marry her because he'd thought it an insult to Tracy. He hadn't really rejected her. The morning in her bed also took on new meaning in the light of later revelations. Neil had drawn back to prevent the hurt that would be sure to follow her discovery that she'd made love to Jake Archer's stepson.

Jake Archer's stepson. Funny how little that mattered now. She'd come to believe Neil's version of their relationship. The magazine article about her father hadn't even mentioned Neil. Even Neil's failure to tell her about it was understandable. He wouldn't have lasted one hour in her house once she'd known the truth. On that subject her attitude had been uncompromisingly irrational.

Tracy propped the ladder against the garage wall. If only she knew how Neil felt about her. Just because her sentiments had changed radically didn't mean that his had. She didn't think that he still despised her, and the fact that he'd put her feelings ahead of his own must show that he cared at least a little for her. But that wasn't enough. She was greedy. Nothing less than Neil's love would satisfy her.

'If you ever need me,' he'd said. What kind of

need had he meant? The kind that cried out for his smiles? The kind that kept her awake at night aching for his kisses and his embrace? The kind that longed to hear his voice, see his face? The kind that admitted that Neil Charles was necessary for her happiness?

All her life people had been dropping into her life, making her love them, and then dropping out again while she stood helplessly by. She'd vowed to never let it happen again. Inside, her house was silent, lonely. Love couldn't be controlled, but that didn't mean she had to submit tamely to fate. The crumpled card with Neil's address and phone number was hidden deep in one of her dresser drawers. She'd retrieved it after he'd left the restaurant.

Did she have the courage? Letting a man know that you loved him made a woman so vulnerable. Could she bear the sadness of discovering that Neil didn't love her? What if he did? Neil's love meant the moon and the stars and happiness beyond belief. Neil had called her a pretty tough broad. Just how tough was she? Tough enough, she decided.

Hand hovering over the telephone, she panicked, cringing at the thought of Neil trying gracefully to explain his lack of interest. Even a letter would force Neil to politely reply. Plagued by doubts and fears, Tracy once more sought solace through her kitchen window.

The young chickadees were splashing in the bird-bath. At the base of the bath yellow columbine nodded cheerfully in the slight breeze. The male bluebird flashed by, bringing a huge grin to Tracy's face. Of course. Neil should hear about the baby bluebirds. A birth announcement demanded no response. Unless he chose to make one. If he didn't. . .Tracy refused to think about that. She would send the announcement. The rest was up to Neil.

She was standing on the ladder when Neil came around the corner of the house. A suit jacket slung over one shoulder, he was jerking off his tie. The sleeves of a rumpled pale blue shirt had been rolled up to his elbows. Weary lines radiated out from his eyes. He was the most beautiful sight she'd ever seen as she clung weakly to the top rung, her knees trembling. Not until now did she admit to herself how frightened she'd been that he wouldn't respond to the card she'd sent him.

He eyed her warily. 'When you didn't answer your doorbell, I thought you might be out here.'

'Would you like to see?' she asked, pointing to the birdhouse with its roof still open to the sky. Her heart was pounding so loudly he must hear it as he came across the lawn.

'What about the other houses?'

'The chickadees had eight babies, and the nuthatches had six. They've all left the nest now, but this morning I saw a house wren at the chickadee house.'

He helped her down the ladder, his head searing the skin on her arm. Looking around, he said, 'I see I missed the lilacs.'

'Yes. They were beautiful this year.' They must have been. She'd never noticed.

He stood on the ladder, peering down into the house. The sun backlit his head; the sky was so intensely blue it hurt her eyes. A humming-bird whistled past her ear *en route* to the geraniums in the front window-box while children's voices drifted across the street from where they played in the neighbour's yard. Nearby a lawn mower was whirring, and the scent of freshly cut grass was in the air. 'Ugly little fellows, aren't they?' Laughter was in his eyes, just as she'd imagined it would be.

Tracy clutched the side of the ladder to support her boneless body. Neil had come back. She laughed, an outlet for the giddy sense of relief that bubbled up within her. 'I'll never complain about the postal service again. I only mailed the card two days ago.'

'What card?' Neil asked.

'The birth announcement. The one about the baby bluebirds. I thought when you got it. . .' Her voice trailed off at the blank look on his face.

Neil climbed down from the ladder and folded it up. He started across the lawn. 'You thought what?'

'I thought you'd want to know about the bluebirds.' Her explanation sounded lame even to her.

He hung the ladder on the garage wall before following her into the kitchen. 'How's the doll's house coming on?'

'Fine.' She flopped down on a chair before her legs collapsed beneath her. Why was Neil here if he hadn't received her card? 'Did my father send you?'

'No.' Neil tossed his jacket over a chair and leaned back against a cabinet, his hands braced on the counter-top on either side of his body. 'He told me you'd called him.' Dark eyes studied her thoughtfully. 'He said you sounded unhappy. Are you?'

'I'm f-fine.'

'I'm glad you are.' He glared down at her. 'I'm not.'

'I'm sorry, I. . .'

'The hell you are. If you were, you'd have done something about it instead of letting me suffer.

Picking up the phone and putting it down a million times over the past three weeks, driving everyone around me crazy, finally building enough courage to fly out here, worrying myself silly during the entire plane trip, rehearsing a million different speeches on the drive down here. . .it's enough to give a man an ulcer.'

'What kind of speeches?'

'The kind that would beg you to forgive me for not being entirely honest with you, the kind that would convince you that I'll do my best to never let you down, the kind that would prove to you that you need me as much as I need you. Damn it, Tracy!' he almost snarled, yanking her up from her chair and pulling her tightly against his hard body. His mouth was buried in her hair. 'I tried to stay away,' he said in a muffled voice. 'I didn't want you to think that I was only coming back because Jake turned over your mother's estate to you. If you don't believe me, you can put the damn thing in a trust for our children.'

'Our children?' She could feel his heart pounding against the palms of her hands.

'Two, I think,' he said, his hands tightening on her shoulders.

'You wouldn't want to overburden the nanny?' She slid her hands up to clasp behind his neck and tipped back her head.

'Exactly,' he said hoarsely, desire darkening his eyes. He captured her mouth, parted her lips, his tongue thrusting fierce and deep. The heat from his body scorched her and liquefied her bones until she no longer had the strength to support herself. She clung to him, her hands buried in his hair, answering kiss with kiss. Disappointment was sharp when his mouth left hers. Neil swept her up into his arms and carried her into the parlour and laid her down. A firm hip nudged her closer to the back of the sofa as he sprawled alongside her, the lower length of his body resting against hers. A sudden draught chilled the upper half of her body as Neil unbuttoned her shirt and edged it away from her shoulders. Her breathing quickened as he brushed aside lacy coverings. Coolness was quickly supplanted by intense heat as Neil's large hand swallowed up one small breast and then the other. Her gasp of pleasure was swallowed by Neil's deep kiss and then he slowly withdrew his lips from hers. 'I've been mad to do this since the morning you attacked me in my sleep,' he said, his voice thick with emotion. He pulled the edges of her blouse together, propped his head on his arm and smiled down into her face.

Tracy nipped his chin with her teeth. 'Your memory's not too good. I was the attackee, not the attacker.'

'Unfortunately, my memory is too good.' He dropped a quick kiss on her lips. 'Behave yourself, we have to talk.'

'About what?'

'Us. About how wrong I was about you.'

She traced the outline of her lips with her finger. 'You mean about me being a typical rich, spoiled brat?'

He bit the tip of her finger. 'That was before I knew you. I quickly discovered that you were far from typical. You were rich all right, not in money but in intangibles like your courage, your dedication to your work, your loyalty to and concern for your friends, your enjoyment of nature, the delightful way your mouth curves when you laugh.' He lowered his head. 'And you spoiled me for any other woman.'

She emerged breathless from the kiss. 'But you left me.'

'You kicked me out. I wanted to stay and force you to admit that you loved me. . .'

'Arrogant male,' Tracy mocked. 'What makes you think I love you?'

'Don't you?'

'Yes, but. . .' When she was free to breathe once more, she asked quickly before he could side-track her again, 'What made you so sure I did?'

'I wasn't exactly sure. Hopeful. The look of betrayal in your eyes that last night almost killed me, but at the same time, it seemed to me that you had to care a little to be so upset. I didn't want to debate the issue then, for fear of forcing you into a position that you'd have too much pride to back down from. You're so damned independent and proud,' he added, the loving tones stripping the words of any censure. 'I wasn't sure you'd see me now, but I just couldn't wait any longer. I missed you so damned much. Have I mentioned yet how much I love you?'

'You haven't mentioned love at all,' she said tartly.

'How could you doubt it? To show up here after you were so cool to me that afternoon in the Rattlesnake grill. I almost lost all hope when you threw away my card.'

'I'm not so proud. I took it back after you left.' She rubbed her cheek against his shoulder. 'I even used it.'

Neil grinned lazily down at her. 'Tell me about the bluebird announcement.'

'There's nothing to tell. I just thought you'd want to know about the babies.'

'Don't you really mean that you couldn't write and tell me that you wanted to see me because I might say no? Rather than risk outright rejection, you managed to come up with a way to let me know that the door was unlocked if I cared to open it.'

'Can I refuse to answer that on the grounds that I might incriminate myself?' she asked. Desire licked along her veins at the laughter in his eyes.

'That does it. You have to marry me.'

She peeked up at him through lowered lashes. 'Who says so? Daddy?'

'Daddy has nothing to do with it.' He rolled so his weight was pressing her into the sofa. 'Just for the record, I might love you because you're an independent woman who's chosen to carve out a career rather than live on her parents' money, or I might love you because you make crazy little houses for Lilliputians, or I might love you because you attack burglars in the night armed with nothing more than a candlestick, or I might love you because the sight of a bluebird in the spring makes you giddy with happiness, or I might even love you because your body drives me wild with desire, but I will never, I repeat, *never*, love you merely because you happen to be Jake Archer's daughter. Is that clear?'

'Might love me?'

'Damn it. *Do* love you.' Neil caught his breath. 'Don't look at me like that.'

'Like what?'

His mouth hovered above hers. 'As if I were your first bluebird of the spring.'

'Or what?' she asked, raising her lips slowly to his.

'Or this.'

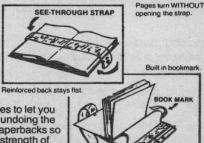

PASSPORT TO ROMANCE VACATION SWEEPSTAKES

OFFICIAL RULES

SWEEPSTAKES RULES AND REGULATIONS. NO PURCHASE NECESSARY.

HOW TO ENTER:

1. To enter, complete this official entry form and return with your invoice in the envelope provided, or print your name, address, telephone number and age on a plain piece of paper and mail to: Passport to Romance, P.O. Box #1397, Buffalo, N.Y. 14269-1397. No mechanically reproduced entries accepted.
2. All entries must be received by the Contest Closing Date, midnight, December 31, 1990 to be eligible.
3. Prizes: There will be ten (10) Grand Prizes awarded, each consisting of a choice of a trip for two people to: i) London, England (approximate retail value $5,050 U.S.); ii) England, Wales and Scotland (approximate retail value $6,400 U.S.); iii) Caribbean Cruise (approximate retail value $7,300 U.S.); iv) Hawaii (approximate retail value $ 9,550 U.S.); v) Greek Island Cruise in the Mediterranean (approximate retail value $12,250 U.S.); vi) France (approximate retail value $7,300 U.S.).
4. Any winner may choose to receive any trip or a cash alternative prize of $5,000.00 U.S. in lieu of the trip.
5. Odds of winning depend on number of entries received.
6. A random draw will be made by Nielsen Promotion Services, an independent judging organization on January 29, 1991, in Buffalo, N.Y., at 11:30 a.m. from all eligible entries received on or before the Contest Closing Date. Any Canadian entrants who are selected must correctly answer a time-limited, mathematical skill-testing question in order to win. Quebec residents may submit any litigation respecting the conduct and awarding of a prize in this contest to the Régie des loteries et courses du Quebec.
7. Full contest rules may be obtained by sending a stamped, self-addressed envelope to: "Passport to Romance Rules Request", P.O. Box 9998, Saint John, New Brunswick, E2L 4N4.
8. Payment of taxes other than air and hotel taxes is the sole responsibility of the winner.
9. Void where prohibited by law.

PASSPORT TO ROMANCE VACATION SWEEPSTAKES

OFFICIAL RULES

SWEEPSTAKES RULES AND REGULATIONS. NO PURCHASE NECESSARY.

HOW TO ENTER:

1. To enter, complete this official entry form and return with your invoice in the envelope provided, or print your name, address, telephone number and age on a plain piece of paper and mail to: Passport to Romance, P.O. Box #1397, Buffalo, N.Y. 14269-1397. No mechanically reproduced entries accepted.
2. All entries must be received by the Contest Closing Date, midnight, December 31, 1990 to be eligible.
3. Prizes: There will be ten (10) Grand Prizes awarded, each consisting of a choice of a trip for two people to: i) London, England (approximate retail value $5,050 U.S.); ii) England, Wales and Scotland (approximate retail value $6,400 U.S.); iii) Caribbean Cruise (approximate retail value $7,300 U.S.); iv) Hawaii (approximate retail value $ 9,550 U.S.); v) Greek Island Cruise in the Mediterranean (approximate retail value $12,250 U.S.); vi) France (approximate retail value $7,300 U.S.).
4. Any winner may choose to receive any trip or a cash alternative prize of $5,000.00 U.S. in lieu of the trip.
5. Odds of winning depend on number of entries received.
6. A random draw will be made by Nielsen Promotion Services, an independent judging organization on January 29, 1991, in Buffalo, N.Y., at 11:30 a.m. from all eligible entries received on or before the Contest Closing Date. Any Canadian entrants who are selected must correctly answer a time-limited, mathematical skill-testing question in order to win. Quebec residents may submit any litigation respecting the conduct and awarding of a prize in this contest to the Régie des loteries et courses du Quebec.
7. Full contest rules may be obtained by sending a stamped, self-addressed envelope to: "Passport to Romance Rules Request", P.O. Box 9998, Saint John, New Brunswick, E2L 4N4.
8. Payment of taxes other than air and hotel taxes is the sole responsibility of the winner.
9. Void where prohibited by law.

 RLS-DIR

VACATION SWEEPSTAKES

MONTH 1 ENTRY

Official Entry Form

Yes, enter me in the drawing for one of ten Vacations-for-Two! If I'm a winner, I'll get my choice of any of the six different destinations being offered — and I won't have to decide until after I'm notified!

Return entries with invoice in envelope provided along with Daily Travel Allowance Voucher. Each book in your shipment has two entry forms — and the more you enter, the better your chance of winning!

Name ______________________________

Address ______________________________ Apt.

City ______________ State/Prov. ______________ Zip/Postal Code

Daytime phone number ______________________________
Area Code

☐ I am enclosing a Daily Travel Allowance Voucher in the amount of $__________ Write in amount revealed beneath scratch-off

- - - - - - - - - - - - - - - - - - - -

PASSPORT
WIN
1 of 10 Vacations
SEE INSIDE
TO ROMANCE.

VACATION SWEEPSTAKES

MONTH 1 ENTRY

Official Entry Form

Yes, enter me in the drawing for one of ten Vacations-for-Two! If I'm a winner, I'll get my choice of any of the six different destinations being offered — and I won't have to decide until after I'm notified!

Return entries with invoice in envelope provided along with Daily Travel Allowance Voucher. Each book in your shipment has two entry forms — and the more you enter, the better your chance of winning!

Name ______________________________

Address ______________________________ Apt.

City ______________ State/Prov. ______________ Zip/Postal Code

Daytime phone number ______________________________
Area Code

☐ I am enclosing a Daily Travel Allowance Voucher in the amount of $__________ Write in amount revealed beneath scratch-off

CPS-ONE